The Con Artist

A Billionaire Romance

Sandi Lynn

Sandi Lynn Romance, LLC

The Con Artist

New York Times, USA Today & Wall Street Journal
Bestselling Author
SANDI LYNN

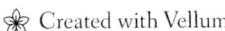 Created with Vellum

Mission Statement

Sandi Lynn Romance

**Providing readers with romance novels that will
whisk them away
to another world and from the daily grind of
life – one book at a time.**

Chapter One

Kate
My eyes were closed, but my mind still planned my next move. My move is to leave Seattle and go home. I slowly opened my eyes as I lay on my side, his arm stretched out over my waist. He was a good man, and my time spent with him was coming to an end. Nigel Thorne was a fifty-year-old millionaire who liked to devour younger women. He'd charm them, use them, and discard them when bored. He became bored quickly, which was good for me because I had no plans to stick around. But he said I was different. Great. He said I was a keeper. Shit. For how long, I didn't know. His first mistake was trusting me. He was a charmer, but I charmed better. He was a seducer, but I had seduced him first. He told me he loved me, and I told him not to be silly. We had only known each other for over two months, just enough time for me to discover his weaknesses and play on them. He bought me expensive handbags, designer clothes, diamond earrings, and a bracelet worth over twenty thousand dollars.

A small smile crossed his lips as his eyes opened and locked on mine. His hand swept through my hair as he leaned in and brushed his mouth against mine.

"Good morning," he whispered.

"Morning," I spoke with a small smile.

"What time is it?" he asked.

"Six thirty."

His chest heaved as he sighed and rolled onto his back, folding his hands behind his head.

"I have a meeting at eight. Don't forget about the dinner party at the Andersons' tonight."

"I haven't forgotten." My finger ran down his chest.

He kissed my forehead before climbing out of bed and hopping into the shower.

"I'll go make some coffee." I slipped on my red satin robe.

"Thank you, darling."

He liked his coffee French pressed. Once finished, I poured some into his favorite brown mug with one cube of sugar and two splashes of skim milk. Taking it into the bathroom, I set the mug on the counter while he stood in front of the mirror and shaved.

"What are your plans for today?" he asked.

"I thought I'd do some shopping. Perhaps buy a new dress for the dinner party tonight."

"Good idea. Make sure it's black, tight, and short." He winked. "Take my credit card and spare no expense."

I had no intention of attending that party because I'd be long gone before he got home from the office. Seattle was nice and all, but my time here was up, and I had other prospects to check out. As I was leaving the bathroom, he called my name.

"Becca?"

"Yes?" I turned around.

"I think you should move in with me."

Ugh. I hated it when they suggested that. Walking over, I placed my hand on his back and stared at him through the mirror.

"We'll discuss that later. If you don't hurry up, you'll be late for your meeting." I smiled.

"I'm in love with you, Becca Wright."

My lips pressed against his bare shoulder before I walked into the bedroom and laid out his suit. He kissed me goodbye once he was dressed and headed out the door. Little did he know that the kiss he gave me would be his last one.

As soon as the front door shut, I showered, dressed, and went into his home office, where I removed the large hunting dog painting that revealed his wall safe. He heavily guarded his combination, and nobody was allowed in his office when he opened it. I had placed a hidden camera amongst the books on the bookshelf across from the painting. Twenty-five left, ten right, five left, six right, and voila. It opened. Inside sat piles of cash, two Rolex watches, a diamond ring that belonged to his grandmother, and important documents that pertained to his business—documents that could ruin him if anyone ever got their hands on them. I placed the three-carat canary diamond on my finger and held my hand out before me. His grandmother raised him his whole life. She was the most important person in the world. I grabbed a few stacks of cash—about a hundred thousand dollars—and the two Rolexes and shut the safe. As I put the painting back on the wall, I stared at his grandmother's ring. Guilt started to wash over me. As much as I wanted to keep the priceless beauty, I knew it would devastate him if it went missing. He was already going to be devastated enough once he found out I had conned him. So, I reopened the safe and placed it back inside the little red velvet box that kept it secure.

I grabbed the small overnight bag that I packed, shoved the money and the watches inside, and headed back to my apartment, which I rented from week to week. I took off my short platinum wig, put on my long brunette one, and called for a cab to take me to the airport.

I checked in and placed my luggage on the scale when I arrived. When I handed the short, stocky man my driver's license, he looked at it and then returned it to me with a smile.

"Have a safe flight to New York, Miss Greaves."

"Thank you." I flashed my pearly whites at him.

I entered the plane, set my carry-on under the seat in front of me, and sank into first-class seat 2D. It always had to be the second row and the window seat. If that seat were sold out, I'd have no problem getting the person who bought it to switch with me. The first row was out of the question because they always made you stow your carry-on. Any rows beyond the second always ran out of the first food choice before the flight attendant reached you. That pissed me off more than anything. And the window? Always the window. It was all about the view, peace, and serenity that I felt when I saw the fluffiness of the clouds that enveloped the sky, not to mention the fact that I hated people climbing over me to get to the bathroom or the food carts bumping me as the flight attendants made their way up and down the aisles.

I lay my head back and took a deep breath, my brunette

wig still in place, and my Chanel sunglasses covered my eyes.

"So, you're the one who booked the window seat?" I heard a man's powerful voice speak.

I turned my head and slightly lowered my sunglasses, only to find a well-tailored black Armani suit staring me in the face. All six foot two of it. I watched as he put his carry-on in the overhead compartment, shut it, and sat beside me. Short, light brown hair that was cut in a classic crew. Simple. Stylish. All American. He had a strong masculine jawline, a perfectly manicured five o'clock shadow, alluring lips, and a pair of men's Phantom Aviator glasses covering his eyes. He radiated a scent. Warm yet cool. Sophisticated. Sea-like with a hint of patchouli. He reeked of wealth.

"Excuse me?" I spoke.

"When I booked this flight, I was disappointed that the window seat was already taken." The corners of his mouth slightly curved upwards.

A rush of warmth flooded my panties, and I swore I'd just had an orgasm.

"When did you book this flight?" I asked.

"Yesterday."

"Then maybe you should have booked it sooner if you wanted the window seat." I smiled.

"Perhaps. But my business in Seattle finished earlier than I expected."

"May I get you a beverage?" the perky young flight attendant asked.

"Tequila with a splash of lime, please," I replied.

"And for you, sir." Her "I want to fuck you" smile widened.

"I'll have a vodka cranberry. Light on the cranberry." He grinned.

I glanced down at his arm, which was sitting on the armrest, and took note of the Cartier watch that sat proudly on his wrist. Elegant, powerful, and out-of-this-world expensive. He didn't remove his sunglasses, nor did I, so I couldn't say anything to him. But I was dying to see his eyes. He wasn't complete until I saw the color of them. Actually, he would never be complete until I saw firsthand what kind of package he was sporting underneath his expensive designer pants. He was the type of man women fell to their knees for, and I could understand why. He was beyond gorgeous. In fact, I don't think my eyes ever laid on anyone sexier. He looked to be in his early thirties, thirty-two at the most.

"Your tequila with a splash of lime." The flight attendant smiled as she handed me my drink.

"Thank you."

"And your vodka cranberry, light on the cranberry." Her grin widened as she handed him his drink with a napkin tucked underneath it.

"Thank you." He flirtatiously smiled back.

Rolling my eyes, I brought my glass to my lips. When he set his napkin down, I noticed she had written her phone number on it with a note that read:

"I'll be in New York for a couple of days. Call me."

I sighed as I set my drink down on it.

"Oh. I'm sorry." I picked it back up. "I would hate for the ink to smear."

He let out a chuckle. Damn it. Even that was hot.

"No worries. And if it did, I wouldn't care."

"She's cute. You wouldn't want to hit that at least once?" I arched my brow.

"She's cute. But she's not my type."

"And what exactly is your type?" I smirked.

"Brunettes with long wavy hair and," he reached over and pulled my glasses from my face, "rich brown eyes."

I stared at him through his Ray-Bans, speechless and gasping for air. Grabbing my glasses from his hand, I slipped them back on.

Chapter Two

Gabriel

The moment I stepped onto the plane and saw the incredibly beautiful woman sitting in the window seat next to mine, my cock started to rise. Long brunette hair with a hint of a wave through it, full sensuous lips, high cheekbones, and a pair of black Chanel sunglasses that framed her face to perfection. Normally, I would ask the person occupying the window seat to switch with me, but something told me that this beauty wouldn't give it up. It was the way she composed herself in her seat. She radiated confidence, and the fact that she kept her sunglasses on indicated she didn't want to be messed with. As I put my carry-on in the overhead compartment, the scent of jasmine and rose overtook my senses. Fresh, seductive, and warm. She had an attitude. I liked it. Telling me I should have booked my flight sooner made me laugh inside. She didn't fumble with her words as most women did in my presence. She was poised and carefully spoken.

"What's your name?" I asked as she took her sunglasses from my hand and put them back on.

"First names only." The corners of her mouth curved up into a small smile. "Hannah."

"It's nice to meet you, Hannah. I'm Gabriel."

"Nice to meet you, Gabe." She cocked her head as she extended her hand.

"Not Gabe. Gabriel. I don't do nicknames." I placed my hand in hers.

"Okay. Now that we've established you don't do nicknames, what do you do?" I noticed her brow arch from underneath her glasses.

"I'm in corporate business. And you?"

"I'm an entrepreneur."

"For what type of business?" I asked for I was intrigued.

"Handbags, jewelry, shoes. Anything that makes a girl feel pretty." She smiled.

Her smile. Illuminating. Radiant. A one-of-a-kind smile. The kind of smile that would turn even the shittiest of days around. My cock was misbehaving, and she would be the perfect woman to punish it.

"Is your business in New York?" I asked.

"No. I'm just visiting a friend for a couple of days."

"I see. Are you going to keep your sunglasses on the whole flight?" I asked.

"Are you? Or are you afraid you will lose power over me and expose your emotional vulnerability?" A smirk crossed her lips.

"I'm sorry?" I shook my head. "What?"

"People who wear sunglasses inside places do it to intimidate people. With that intimidation comes power. And that power is a mask for the emotional vulnerability that you possess. Or it could simply mean that you want to create an aura of mystery about yourself, leaving people to guess what's hiding beneath those glasses."

Shit. What the fuck?

"So, which is it, Gabriel? Emotional vulnerability or mystery?"

"I could ask you the same thing, Hannah," I replied with an arch in my brow.

She let out a light laugh. "I'm wearing them because I'm tired, and the darkness of the shades will help me sleep.

"Then, by all means, get some rest. I'll wake you when we land."

"Thank you. You still haven't answered my question."

I sighed as I stared at her.

"And I'm not going to."

"I'm going to go with emotional vulnerability." She reclined her seat and turned her head towards the window.

Did she even realize to whom she was speaking? Something told me that this one was out of control with her mouth. But yet, I found her irresistible. As she slept, I stared at her. My eyes raked over the gray cardigan she wore with the black tank top underneath and tight black pants. I needed to see her standing up. My mind only imagined what was hiding under those layers of clothes. Her face was beautiful, and I would bet my life that her body was just as sexy. Once again, my cock started to rise just thinking about me fucking her from behind, gripping her ass as tight as I could while I pounded in and out of her, listening to the screams of her ecstasy as my cock satisfied her every need.

I hadn't had great sex in a while. Greta, my new ex-girlfriend, had become unbelievably irritating, always whining and bitching at me for something. She'd bitch when I had to work late and then tell her mom and sister what a horrible boyfriend I was because I didn't spend enough time with her. We'd been dating for six months, and for me, it was six months too long. Withholding sex was her form of punishment for me. Did I care? Not really. We'd been broken up for twenty-four hours, and it had been the best twenty-four hours of my life. I had no choice but to dump her when I was in Seattle. I couldn't take her calling me every half hour and then blowing up my phone with ridiculous text messages asking me whom I was sleeping with because I didn't answer. I'd never cheated on her. I didn't do shit like that. It wasn't who I was. Even though I was a powerful, wealthy man, I still respected my relationships with women. It was her insecurities that led her to think I was sleeping around with every woman in the world. Ha. I wished.

When I wasn't in a relationship, I found I was better off not being in one. I'd have a lot of sex with different women. One-night stands mainly. Women I met at business conferences, bars, restaurants, and business trips—all casual, no strings, and absolutely perfect. I got my needs fulfilled without all the bullshit drama. I made a vow that once I got rid of Greta and she was out of my life, I would stay single for a long time. Even if the right woman appeared right before me, it didn't matter. I was tired of all the harping. It exhausted me, and work did that enough. Running a multi-billion-dollar hotel and resort chain wasn't easy. There was too much competition out there, and I needed to keep on top of my game if I wanted to remain the best.

I was the CEO of Quinn Hotels. Our chain was right up there with Four Seasons, Ritz Carlton, and Mandarin Oriental. Last year, Forbes placed Quinn Hotels, also known as "Q," number four on their list of the ten best hotel chains in the world. I inherited the company when my father passed away two years ago. He inherited it from his father, my grandfather, who started the luxurious hotel chain back in 1929 and quickly became a huge competitor for Hilton Hotels.

My work was my life, and the women I dated needed to understand that. Greta swore she did, which I believed for the first month of our relationship. Then the arguing started and all the crying. That woman cried a river more than anyone I'd ever known. She stressed me out more than she made me happy. Why didn't I dump her sooner? I had a lot going on, and breaking up with her seemed more trouble than it was worth at the time. Piss poor excuse, I know. But I was in the middle of opening a new hotel. We ran into many problems, and I didn't want to deal with her.

Chapter Three

K ate

The bumpiness of the plane landing jolted me out of my seat.

"What the hell? Doesn't this pilot know how to land a plane?"

Gabriel chuckled. "It wasn't that bad."

"Says you. You weren't in the middle of a dream on the beach, soaking up the sun and being served fruity drinks with cute little umbrellas by an incredibly sexy guy."

"No. I wasn't. And I'd be overly concerned if I was." He smirked.

His smirk made me tighten my legs. I didn't mention that the incredibly sexy guy serving me drinks on the beach was him. I'd just met him, and he was already invading my dreams. My eyes couldn't stop diverting themselves to his shiny watch. The plane finally stopped, and the captain spoke over the speaker.

"There will be a thirty-minute delay in retrieving your luggage from baggage claim. It appears that some of the carousels are not working at the moment, and there's a backup of luggage from other flights that will be put through first."

"Are you fucking kidding me?" I sighed as I stood up from my seat.

"Do you have somewhere to be?" Gabriel asked.

"Of course. Don't you?" I cocked my head at him as we exited the plane.

"Yes, but it's only thirty minutes," he replied. "How about we get a drink while we wait?"

"I think a drink would be fine since I'm not going anywhere anytime soon." I smiled.

I needed that watch.

We entered the Delta Sky Lounge, ordered our drinks, and sat on a bright red couch. When Gabriel removed his glasses, I felt the air in my lungs constrict. A rich chocolate brown. Seductive. The kind of eyes that could burn a hole through your very soul.

"So, what do you do in the corporate world?" I asked.

"A lot of shit that makes my head go crazy." He grinned. "Where is your store located?"

"Cyber World."

"Ah, you're an online retailer?" His brow arched.

"Yes." I smiled.

"What's the name?" he asked.

"Why do you want to know?"

"Why not?"

"So you can stalk me?" I gave him a sly smile.

Our eyes were fixated on each other, and the sexual chemistry between us was on fire. He wanted to fuck me as badly as I wanted his watch.

"I wouldn't stalk you. I'm just curious." He brought his hand up to my cheek.

"I'm sure you have someone waiting at home for you," I spoke.

"I don't."

"Someone as sexy as you is single?"

"Yes." His hand ran down my cheek.

I gulped at the fierce vibrating down below.

"How about you?" he asked, placing his hand between my legs.

"No. I don't have anyone."

"Someone as beautiful as you is single?"

"That's right." I smiled.

He took his thumb and ran it across my lips. As a reaction, I took it in my mouth.

"Fuck, Hannah. We need to go into the bathroom."

"Lead the way." I smiled.

He grabbed my hand and led me down the small hallway where the bathroom was. As soon as we were both inside, he shut the door and locked it. Suddenly, his hands grabbed the sides of my face, and his mouth smashed into mine without warning. I stumbled back as he held on to me with one arm wrapped around me. Our lips tangled, and our tongues greeted each other. This was what you called an unexpected, heated moment. Sliding his suit coat off his shoulders, I quickly unbuttoned his crisp white shirt as his hands slid off my cardigan and then dipped down the front of my shirt, groping my breasts as subtle moans escaped him. He broke our kiss and took down his pants. Thank God he was so blessed in the goods department. Thick, long, hard, and beautiful. I was going to have an orgasm just looking at it.

"Like what you see?" He smirked.

"Definitely." I licked my lips.

He placed his hands on my hips and turned me around

before pulling down my pants and pressing his hard cock against me.

"I want you to watch me fuck you in the mirror," he seductively spoke as he dipped his finger inside me.

I threw my head back in desire as he explored my insides.

"You're so wet. Are you ready for me?" he asked as he ripped a condom package open and rolled it over his cock.

"Yes," I spoke breathlessly as my body prepared for his entrance.

He thrust inside me. Hard. Deep. The feel of him was intoxicating, and I was getting drunk with each stroke. His grip on my hips tightened as he pounded into me, making me voice the pleasure I felt. I looked at him through the mirror, and our eyes met.

"Don't look away when you come," he spoke.

My body was pushed to the limits, and the minute he reached his hand over and placed it on top of my clit, an orgasm rushed through me.

"That's it. God, that's it," he panted.

One last hard thrust and he halted while deep moans escaped him as he came.

I reached my hand around and placed it on the back of his head as his lips pressed against my shoulder. He pulled out, removed the condom, and tossed it in the trashcan. He bent down, pulled up my pants, and then groped my breasts one last time. I picked up my cardigan, slipped it on, and took hold of his wrist before he put on his suit coat. He looked at me as I brought my other hand up to his cheek.

"Thank you." I smiled as my lips tenderly met his.

"You're welcome."

I let go of his wrist and slipped his watch into the pocket of my cardigan. Now, I needed to quickly exit before he noticed it was gone. We walked out of the bathroom together and out of the lounge.

"It was nice to meet you, Gabriel." I smiled as I walked the opposite way.

"Baggage claim is this way?" He pointed.

"I have a quick phone call to make first. Thanks again." I bit down on my bottom lip.

"The pleasure was all mine, Hannah." He winked.

I knew JFK like the back of my hand since I traveled so much and went another way to get to baggage claim. When I arrived, I hid around the corner and waited for him to retrieve his luggage. Once he did and began to walk away, I swallowed hard as I silently whispered, "Goodbye, Gabriel." After he left the airport, I grabbed my bags and headed the opposite way, where I hailed a cab and went home.

Chapter Four

G abriel
My bag was coming around the carousel when I arrived. I felt a little off by what had happened, and I didn't want to walk away. She was incredible, and I needed to know more about her. But she said she was only in New York for a few days. It was time I put Hannah out of my mind because I'd never see her again.

"Good evening, Carl," I spoke as I climbed into the back of my limo.

"Good evening, sir. How was Seattle?"

"Rainy." I smiled. "But productive."

"Home, sir?" he asked.

"Yes."

I turned my wrist to look at the time on my watch, and it wasn't there.

"What the hell?" I loudly spoke.

"Is something wrong, Mr. Quinn?"

I never took my watch off. I distinctly remembered it being on my wrist while I was fucking her.

"That bitch stole my watch!"

"Excuse me, sir?" Carl spoke.

"Nothing." I climbed out of the car. "I'll be right back. I have to look for someone."

I raced back to baggage claim and looked around for Hannah. Looking at the carousel where our luggage had come from, it was empty. I stepped outside and looked around. Nothing. She wasn't anywhere to be found. I climbed back into the limo and told Carl to take me home.

I was enraged. A thirty-thousand-dollar watch gone— taken by a woman I met on an airplane and fucked in the sky lounge at JFK airport. How stupid could I be? Fuck! I pulled my ringing phone from my pocket and saw it was Greta calling. What the hell did she want? I wasn't in any mood to deal with her, so I sent her to voicemail.

Carl pulled up to my building at 178 East 94th Street, a townhome I had purchased three years ago when it went into foreclosure. My family and friends were shocked when I purchased it because they always believed I was a high-rise penthouse type of man. The thing I liked most was the homey feel it had. It was a place I felt would be right to have a family someday in the distant future. Or at least that was what I saw three years ago. Since then, my views on family and marriage had drastically changed thanks to the crazy women I'd dated.

As soon as I stepped through the front door, Grace, my housekeeper, greeted me.

"Welcome home, Gabriel," she spoke as she took my suitcase from me.

"Thanks, Grace. How's everything going?"

"Well, your ex-girlfriend stopped by earlier and cried her eyes out to me, mumbling something about what an asshole you are and how you broke up with her over the phone."

I rolled my eyes. "Sorry about that."

"Don't be. The only thing I heard was you breaking up with her." She smiled. "Don't get me wrong. She was okay, but she sure whined and cried a lot."

"I know." I sighed.

"I'm going to take your suitcase upstairs and then head home. There's dinner warming in the oven if you're hungry."

"Thanks, Grace. I appreciate it."

"No problem. I'll see you tomorrow."

I took a glass and a bottle of bourbon, went upstairs, and sat on the terrace. Pulling out my phone, I called my little brother, Caleb.

"Hey, big brother, how was Seattle?" he answered.

"It was good. What are you doing?"

"Packing. I leave for Los Angeles tomorrow."

"Ah. That's right. Do you have time to stop by for a drink?"

"Sure. Give me about an hour, and I'll be over."

"Sounds good. I can send Carl to pick you up," I spoke by mistake.

"Really, Gabriel?"

"Sorry. I'll see you in about an hour. I'm up on the terrace."

Caleb Quinn, my twenty-four-year-old, determined-to-be-a-rock-star brother, was against anything money. I guess you could say he had always been the family's black sheep, at least in my father's eyes. He hated wealth and wanted nothing to do with upper-class society, including father's company. I was all about business adventures, while he was all about the music. He had music in his soul, and it showed every time he picked up his guitar. Our father was a tough man with a dream of both his sons running the family company. When my brother graduated high school and threw away a college opportunity to pursue music, my father practically disowned him, calling him a disgrace to the Quinn name. I didn't care what Caleb did or didn't do. He was my brother, and I loved him.

"Hey, bro," Caleb spoke as he leaned down and hugged me before taking a seat across from me.

"Hey, Caleb. Drink?" I asked.

"You got any beer up here?"

I chuckled. "Only for you."

I stood up from the couch, walked over to the minibar on the terrace, and grabbed him a beer.

"What time is your flight tomorrow?" I asked.

"Eight a.m. Where's Greta? I figured she would have been here since you just got home."

I sighed. "I broke things off with her."

"Wow. When?"

"A couple of days ago."

"While you were in Seattle?" He laughed.

"I couldn't take it anymore."

"Yeah. I get that. She was a whiner and very insecure. I never understood what you saw in her." He held up his bottle of beer. "Here's to both the Quinn brothers being single again." He smiled.

"Touché." I lightly tapped my glass against his bottle.

I was embarrassed by what happened at the airport and debated whether to tell Caleb until he noticed I wasn't wearing my watch.

"Where's your watch? You never take it off."

I took in a deep, relentless breath.

"You're never going to believe what happened."

"Don't tell me you lost it." He kicked back his beer.

"It was stolen."

"Stolen? The maid at the hotel?" He cocked his head.

"No. By a woman whom I met on the plane home and fucked in the bathroom in the sky lounge at JFK."

A roar of laughter came from him.

"Shut the fuck up!" He continued laughing. "You left it on the sink, and then she took it, right?"

"No. She took it right off my wrist, and I didn't know it until I got in the car to come home," I spoke with irritation.

"Jesus Christ, Gabriel. How did you let that happen?" He continued to laugh. "I mean, come on, bro, she just slipped it right off your wrist without you knowing?"

"Yep."

"Damn, she must have been one hell of a fuck for you to space out like that. Just call her up and ask her for it back."

"I would, but I don't have her number."

"Ah." He finished off his beer. "Did you at least get her name?"

"Hannah, and that's all I know about her except that she runs some women's online retail shop. She doesn't even live in New York. She said she's only visiting a friend for a couple of days."

He tipped his empty beer bottle toward me. "You, big brother, got ripped off by a chick who's sitting pretty with a thirty-thousand-dollar Cartier watch."

"Do me a favor, and don't say a word about this to anyone. This little mishap stays between us."

"Don't worry. I'm way too embarrassed for you to talk about it." He grinned. "Thanks for the beer." He stood up. "I better get going. I have a few things to wrap up before me and the band head to L.A. tomorrow."

I pulled a few hundred-dollar bills from my wallet and placed them in Caleb's hand.

"Gabriel, I don't—"

"I don't care if you don't need it. Just take it. Please. I've been through enough today, and you turning it down will make me feel worse."

He let out a heavy sigh.

"Thanks," he spoke as he hugged me.

"You're welcome. Good luck with Sony Records tomorrow. I know you'll nail a contract." I smiled.

"I hope so. I'll call you when I get back." He flicked his finger under my chin. "Cheer up, buttercup. The bright side is you can afford to go out tomorrow and buy another one."

I gave him a small smile, and as he was leaving the terrace, he turned and looked at me.

"I know it's not actually about the watch, bro."

I picked up the bottle of bourbon and poured one last glass for the night. As I stood and looked out at the East River amid the brightly lit city, I knew he was right. It wasn't so much about the watch as it was about the woman who stole it from me.

Chapter Five

Kate

When the cab pulled up to 16 East 84th Street, I climbed out and stared at the five-story brick building. It felt good to be home.

"Here's your luggage, ma'am," the cab driver spoke.

"Thank you." I smiled as I reached into my purse and paid him along with a generous tip.

I rolled my suitcase behind me as I climbed into the elevator and took it to my apartment on the fifth floor. Inserting the key into the lock, I pushed open the door and turned on the light switch in the hallway. Brown boxes were scattered all over the place, waiting to be unpacked. I had only been in my new place for three nights before I left for Seattle.

I moved from Chicago to Manhattan to be closer to my dad. When I was a little girl, we moved around a lot, never staying in one place for more than six months or less than a year at a time. I never had any friends because we never stuck around long enough for me to make any connections with anyone. When I was eighteen, we moved to Chicago.

My dad said it could be a permanent place for us, and if the job he would do in New York panned out, we could stay, and I could go to college. But he got involved with the wrong people, costing him twenty years at Rikers Island.

I threw my carry-on bag on the bed and started unpacking it. Pulling Gabriel's watch from my cardigan pocket, I held it in my hand and thought of him. A feeling swept over me, and thoughts about our encounter in the bathroom sent shivers down my spine. In fact, it wasn't just thoughts about what happened. It was thoughts about him in general. Shaking my head, I returned to reality and unpacked my luggage. I couldn't think about him. I didn't want to think about him. I had other things to do. Business. It was now always about the business. I had six rules I lived by.

Know your mark.
Listen and never look bored.
Never reveal your true self.
Never stay in one place too long.
Exit as smoothly as you entered.
Never fall in love.

Everything I did, I did alone. I didn't trust anyone. How could I when I couldn't even trust myself? This wouldn't be my life. It was just long enough until I paid off his debt. I visited my dad once a month, no matter where I was. It was important to him and me. He was all I had left in this world. I lived out of hotels most of the time, and sometimes, I rented an apartment week to week, depending on how long I would be in one place.

I had been lying to him for the past six years. He believed I had been living in Chicago, working as a waitress in an upscale restaurant, and paying my way through college, taking part-time classes. If he knew the truth, he'd be disappointed. He was the last person I wanted to disappoint.

One Month Later

I placed the long, burgundy-colored wig with the loose curls on my head and secured it. After popping the emerald green contacts into my eyes, I dressed in a low-cut, short, black sleeveless dress and slipped my feet into a pair of Jimmy Choo peep-toe black heels with red bottoms. Grabbing my red evening bag from the dresser, I hailed a cab to The Plaza Hotel, where Samuel Coldwater was picking me up. He believed I was staying there until I found a permanent place to live. I waited inside and watched out the lobby doors for his limo to pull up to the curb. Once I saw him climb out, I met him on the sidewalk.

"Amy, you look simply stunning." He smiled as he took hold of my hand and brought it up to his lips.

"So do you, darling," I spoke as he helped me into the car.

"I was going to come up and get you. You didn't have to wait in the lobby."

"I was ready earlier than planned, so I thought I'd save you the trip up." I smiled.

We were heading to the Champagne & Diamonds Winter Gala at the Mandarin Oriental, which his company, Coldwater Enterprises, was hosting. It was a charity event to support and develop a women's center for specialty care.

The Celeste Coldwater Center was to be named after his wife, who passed away over a year ago.

"I want to give you something." He smiled as he reached into his coat pocket and pulled out a small blue box from Tiffany.

"Samuel, you shouldn't have."

"Just open it, darling."

I untied the white ribbon and opened the box. Reaching inside, I pulled out a velvet blue ring box and slowly lifted the lid.

"Samuel. Oh my god. It's beautiful."

He took the white gold, round-cut pink diamond ring with smaller pink diamonds out of the box and placed it on my right ring finger.

"It looks gorgeous on you, Amy." He brought my hand to his lips.

"Samuel, I can't accept this. It's too much. We haven't known each other that long." Tears sprang to my eyes—on-command tears I had mastered over the years. The same tears I used to use on my father when it suited the situation.

"Nothing is too much for you, darling. You're very special to me, and I want you to know just how much." He caressed my cheek.

Leaning in, I brushed my lips against his.

"You're special to me too. Thank you."

The limo pulled up to the Mandarin Oriental, and we stepped inside and headed to the grand ballroom where the event was taking place. Guests had already started to fill the room. All of Manhattan's upper-class society was there. Women were dripping in diamonds, and men reeked of Cartier, Rolex, and diamond cuff links.

"May I get you a glass of champagne?" Samuel asked.

"A glass of champagne would be nice. Thank you." I smiled.

Samuel Coldwater, founder and CEO of Coldwater Enterprises, was worth millions. He was a fifty-five-year-old man who stood approximately six feet two with salt and pepper hair. He was in great shape for his age and a man who took his looks very seriously. I wasn't the first woman he'd dated since his wife passed, but I was the youngest.

I walked around the room and mingled with Samuel's guests, accidentally bumping into men who quickly forgave me with a glorious "I would love to fuck you" smile. A smile that would soon turn to frustration once they discovered their wallet, watches, and other valuables were missing in the morning.

Chapter Six

G abriel

I was standing by the bar talking to a friend of mine, Owen Gray, when a woman with curly brown hair in a red low-cut dress invaded our space.

"Hey there, handsome." She smiled.

"Hello." I smiled back.

"Is that bourbon you're drinking?"

"It is. Would you like one?"

"I'd love one." She batted her eyes. "I'm Tash Cummings." She held out her hand with her well-manicured fingers.

"Gabriel Quinn," I politely spoke as I placed my hand in hers.

Owen excused himself to the restroom and left Tash and me to talk alone. As she went on about her ex-boyfriend, my eyes glanced around the ballroom in boredom. I needed to find a way to escape this woman politely. That was when I noticed a woman with long, burgundy-colored hair in an elegant black dress heading towards the bar. She captivated me.

"Excuse me, Gabriel. Are you even listening to me?" Tash asked with irritation.

My eyes snapped back to hers. "Yes. I'm sorry. Please excuse me for a moment. A friend of mine just walked in that I haven't seen in a very long time. We'll catch up later." I smiled as I placed my hand on her arm and walked away.

As I walked towards her, she was stopped by another woman, and they began a conversation. I halted a few feet back—that smile. I gulped. It couldn't be. She finished her conversation, and I followed behind her to the bar.

"What can I get you, miss?" the bartender asked.

"Tequila with a splash of lime, please."

I could feel the anger rise through my body as I clenched my fists. I couldn't let her see me. Not yet. Not here in front of all these people. I'd follow her and wait until she was alone before I confronted her and possibly killed her. I walked to the other side of the ballroom, never taking my eyes off her, watching her every move. Samuel walked up to her and kissed her cheek. What the fuck? Was she with him? She hooked her arm in his as he led her to their table for dinner. I sat at a table with some friends across the room, far enough away but close enough to keep an eye on her.

"No date tonight, Gabriel?" my friend Jordan asked.

"Actually, the woman I was supposed to bring has the flu. And speaking of dates, who is that woman with Samuel?"

"I have no clue, but he's sure one lucky bastard. She's gorgeous. I'd fuck her until my dick went numb." Jordan grinned.

"All I know is her name is Amy, and he's head over heels for her," Owen said. "He bought her this gorgeous twenty-thousand-dollar pink diamond ring at Tiffany."

"He told you that?" I asked.

"I was in there buying a bracelet for Kitty's birthday, and I ran into him. He was really excited to give it to her."

"I see," I spoke as I stared across the room at her.

Samuel got up and exited the ballroom. I suspected he was headed to the men's room, so I followed him.

"Hello there, Samuel," I spoke as I took the urinal beside him.

"Good to see you, Gabriel. Thank you for coming."

"No problem. Anything for a good cause. I couldn't help but admire your date tonight."

"Ah, yes. That's Amy. Isn't she a beauty? She's so smart and elegant. She's a keeper, that one. I haven't been this happy since before Celeste passed away."

"Yes. She is very beautiful. You're a lucky man, Samuel." I smiled.

"I sure am, Gabriel." He winked.

∽

Kate

I was eating dinner, and when Samuel got up and excused himself to the restroom, I glanced across the room and saw a gorgeous-looking man in a black tux heading out the ballroom doors. What the hell? Shit. It couldn't be. A nervousness settled inside me. What was he doing here? I needed to remain calm. There was no way he could recognize me. I looked totally different from that day on the plane: different hair, different colored eyes, and a different nose. But I couldn't take the chance, so I needed to escape and get out of there. I waited and watched as Gabriel and Samuel walked back into the ballroom together. Shit. What if Samuel brought him over and introduced us? I started to feel sick. I wasn't just a fuck at the airport. I was the fuck who stole his thirty-thousand-dollar Cartier watch. Samuel sat beside me, and I gently placed my hand on his.

"I'm not feeling well. If it's okay with you, I'm going to head back to the hotel."

"What's wrong, darling?" he asked with concern.

"I'm just a little lightheaded. My stomach doesn't feel very good, either. I'm worried I may be coming down with something."

"Then let's go. You need to lie down and rest."

"You stay," I spoke. "This is your event, and you're the host. You can't leave."

"But I'm worried about you."

"Thank you, Samuel. I appreciate it, but I'll be fine. If I need anything, I'll call you." I gently smiled.

"All right. I'll have Bruno bring the limo around." He kissed my cheek.

∼

Gabriel

I saw her get up from her seat and head out the ballroom doors, so I followed her. I assumed she was heading to the restroom but went outside the hotel doors and stood at the curb. Pulling my phone from my pocket, I called Carl to bring the limo around. I waited inside and watched a different limo pull up, and she climbed inside alone. As the limo was pulling away, Carl pulled up. I hurried and climbed inside, telling him to follow that limo and be discreet.

Her limo pulled up to The Plaza Hotel, and she climbed out and went inside. I needed to get her alone, so I planned to follow her up to her room. But before I could climb out of the limo, she returned and hailed a cab. What the hell was she doing?

"Follow that cab, Carl."

"Yes, sir."

The cab pulled up alongside the curb of an apartment building, and she climbed out.

"Carl, follow her and grab the door when she opens it."

Carl did as I asked, and as soon as she entered the building, I stepped out of the limo and followed her to the elevator. This was my chance. The doors began to close, so I stuck my hand in between to stop them. When they opened, our eyes locked on each other's. Emerald green instead of brown. It had to be her. If it wasn't, I was in deep shit.

"Hello." I smiled, playing it off as if I didn't know her.

"Hello." She looked away from me.

I stepped inside the elevator and noticed she pushed the button to the fifth floor.

"Which floor?" she asked.

"Same as you."

She was nervous. I could smell it and tell by how she stared straight ahead and lightly tapped her foot on the ground.

"You're very beautiful," I spoke.

"If you're thinking about trying something, you better think twice," she replied.

I silently laughed to myself. That fucking attitude. It was her, all right. The second the doors shut, I placed my hand around her neck and pushed her up against the elevator wall.

"You have something of mine, and I want it back!" I spoke through gritted teeth as I stared into her calm eyes.

"I don't know what you're talking about."

My grip around her tightened. "I think you do, Hannah." I cocked my head.

"The name is Amy. You obviously have the wrong person."

The elevator doors opened, and I released her but quickly grabbed hold of her arm with a tight grip.

"Let go of me, you psychotic asshole!" She struggled to get away from me.

"This is what we're going to do. We're going to your apartment, and you'll tell me exactly who you are."

She turned her head, spit in my face, broke free from my grip, kneed me in the balls, and ran down the hallway.

"Fuck!" I grabbed my crotch and threw my head back.

I ran after her just as she made it inside her apartment, and as she tried to close the door, I pushed it harder, and she fell back. Stepping inside, I closed the door and locked it.

"What do you want, Gabriel? You want to fuck me again?" she asked angrily as she crawled backward on the floor away from me.

"No, sweetheart. I don't. I want my watch back. As soon as I get it, I'll leave."

She took in a deep breath and got up from the floor. She appeared to have calmed down. I couldn't stop staring at her long, lean legs and killer body as she took off her shoes.

Chapter Seven

Kate

"Listen, I'm sorry about your watch," I spoke as I took my shoes to my bedroom and threw them in the closet.

"Sorry? You're sorry? Is that all you can say? I want my fucking watch back!" he shouted.

"I wish I could give it to you, but I can't."

"What do you mean you can't?" he spoke through gritted teeth.

I went to leave the bedroom, and as I walked past him, he grabbed my arm.

"Again. What do you mean you can't?"

"I sold it. Okay?"

He let go of my arm and placed his hands on his head.

"You sold it?" he spoke in a calm tone. "Who the fuck are you?"

"Someone you should never have trusted," I replied as I walked out of the bedroom and into the kitchen for a glass of wine.

He didn't follow me out of the bedroom, which

concerned me. I needed him out of my apartment. While pouring a glass of wine, I heard various noises from the bedroom. When I ran to see what was going on, he was in the middle of ransacking my room. All my dresser drawers were opened, and my lingerie and clothes were all over the floor.

"What do you think you're doing?" I yelled when I found him in my closet, grabbing the black leather briefcase I had hidden on a shelf behind my long dresses.

"What's with all the wigs, Hannah?"

"Give me that!" I tried to grab the briefcase from his hand, but he pushed me back, and I fell against the closet door.

He threw it on the bed and opened it.

"What the fuck?" He turned his head and looked at me. "Hannah Greaves. Amy Frankel, Becca Wright, Thea Turner, Gizelle Carrington." He rattled off each name as he threw my passports one by one onto the bed. "Jenny Smith, Briana Holmes, Diana Vermander, Nicole Potts. My God. I can't believe this."

"I'm calling the police," I spoke as I got up. "And I'm pressing charges against you for assault."

"Go ahead. I won't be the only one going to jail." He glared at me as he sat on the bed and folded his hands.

I stood there with my back up against the wall, plotting my next move. There had to be a way out of this. Suddenly, he jumped up from the bed and hastily walked to the hallway, where I had my purse sitting on the table. I chased him and tried to grab it, but it was too late.

"You're just a common little thief. Did you take all of this tonight?" His eyes narrowed at me as he dumped the contents of my purse on the floor.

I looked away as I stood there with my arms crossed.

"And Samuel?" he asked. "What were you hoping to get out of him? Did he give you that ring you're wearing? Is that what you do? You find rich men, get them to fall in love with you, and then rip them off?" he shouted. "Answer me!"

I remained calm. I could get out of this situation because I was good. He wanted me once before, and I knew he couldn't resist me now. Walking over to him, I ran my finger down his chest.

"We can work this out," I said seductively.

I leaned in and attempted to brush my lips against his, but he grabbed hold of both my arms and pushed me away.

"You bet we're going to work this out. Pack a bag. You're coming with me."

"Excuse me? Where?"

"To my house."

"You're crazy. I'm not leaving with you."

"One night. That's all I ask." His demeanor and tone of voice changed. "One night for thirty thousand dollars. If you agree to sleep with me, I will forget all of this, and we'll part ways and never see each other again."

"Why?" I asked suspiciously.

"Because you look incredible in that dress. It's a miracle that I'm seeing you again, and I never once stopped thinking about our encounter at the airport."

He slowly walked towards me and ran his hand down my cheek.

"I want you to stay with me for the night. It's the least you can do to repay me for the watch you stole."

"Then you can stay here at my place tonight," I spoke.

"I'm more comfortable at my place. Plus, I would like to try a couple of things with you there. After all, I must ensure I get my thirty-thousand dollars' worth." He smirked.

I gulped. He was kinky, and I found myself turned on. I hadn't stopped thinking about him since that day and couldn't even say why.

He leaned in and softly brushed his lips against mine, nipping at my bottom lip and parting my lips with his tongue. My body was on fire, and I wanted him inside me again.

"That's a pretty expensive night," I spoke breathlessly.

"I know it'll be worth it. I'm a man with many needs—needs I know you can fulfill. As I said, I can't seem to stop thinking about that day at the airport." His hands ran up the back of my dress and grabbed hold of my ass. "You have to admit. We were good together."

"Fine. But I leave in the morning," I spoke as I ran my hand over the bulge in his pants.

"That's fine. I'd want you to leave anyway."

His tongue traveled to my neck and slid down to my cleavage. My lower half was on fire, and I needed him to fan the flames.

"Now, let's go pack you a bag," he spoke as he led me back into the bedroom.

This was my only way out. I would spend the night with him and then leave in the morning. Once I returned home, I would pack up everything and move out of New York. It was too risky to stay here any longer.

Chapter Eight

Gabriel
I took the bag from her and held out my arm. She hooked hers around mine, and we walked out of the building and climbed into the limo. Carl looked at me through the rearview mirror.

"Home, Carl."

"Yes, sir."

I reached over and grabbed hold of her hand, interlaced our fingers, and stared at the ring Samuel gave her. She looked over at me with a small smile. She was playing me, but in the end, she'd be the one to lose the game.

When Carl pulled the limo to the curb in front of my townhome, she leaned over me and stared at it through the window.

"Is this it?" she asked.

"Yes. Is there a problem with it?"

"No. I just figured a man like you would be living in a penthouse in a high-rise luxury building."

"I like my townhome. It's cozy." I smirked.

I opened the door and helped her out of the limo. Grabbing her bag, I held my arm out and walked her to the front door. Once we stepped inside, I let her look around.

"Wow. This is beautiful, Gabriel."

"Thank you. Like I said, it's cozy. Shall we go upstairs?" I held out my hand.

"Of course." She smiled. "How many floors are in this house?"

"Six. My bedroom is on the fifth," I lied.

My bedroom was the entire fourth floor, and the fifth floor consisted of three guest bedrooms, each with an adjoining bathroom. I led her to the room decorated in gray and plum colors.

"After you." I held out my hand.

She walked into the bedroom and looked around. Setting her purse on the dresser, she spoke, "This seems small for a master bedroom."

"I need to run downstairs and grab something. I'll be right back."

"Okay. I'm going to freshen up in the bathroom." She smiled.

I placed her bag on the floor and grabbed her purse from the dresser. Walking out of the bedroom, I shut the door and locked it from the outside. Running down to Carl, I handed him her keys from her purse.

"Go back to her apartment, grab the briefcase on her bed, and bring it back to me."

"Sir?" He cocked his head.

"No questions, Carl. I will be giving you a large cash bonus for doing this."

I could hear the pounding on the door coming from the fifth floor. Rolling my eyes, I returned and politely asked her to stop.

"Let me out of here, Gabriel!" she screamed.

"No can do, sweetheart. Your first mistake was stealing from me, and your second mistake was trusting me." I smiled as I walked away.

~

K ate

I couldn't believe this. He tricked me, and I fucking fell for it. Damn it! I needed to get out of here. I pulled on the knob and continued to pound on the door, yelling obscenities. Walking over to the window, I lifted it, but it stopped a few inches above the sill. Damn those fucking child safety windows. I could scream out the window, hoping the neighbors would hear me, but if they called the cops, I'd go to jail with him. He'd send them to my apartment, and they'd find all my fake passports. I was trapped in this beautifully decorated room with only a TV for entertainment. I was so exhausted by the events of the night. He couldn't leave me in here. He'd be back in the morning to let me out. I knew he would. I decided to make the best of my situation and take a hot bath in the oversized Jacuzzi tub to plan my next move.

~

G abriel

The pounding and relentless yelling stopped. She called me every name in the book and then some. I sat on the couch with a bourbon in my hand. What was I going to do with her? I wanted my watch or the money back. This little con artist was going to learn that it wasn't nice to steal from people. As I sat there sipping my drink, I wondered what she was doing. Why did I care? Was she crying? Doubted it. From what I could tell, she didn't have a sensitive bone in her body. It was apparent she made a living by conning people, and Samuel Coldwater was her latest victim. She was incredibly smart, and it was a shame she wasted her intelligence by doing what she did. Actually, it made me sick.

~

K ate
    Before climbing into the tub, I removed my wig and let down my long blonde hair. When I took out my colored contacts, my eyes returned to the blue color they were. I leaned over the sink, pulled off my latex prosthetic nose, and set it on the counter. Looking in the mirror, I stared at my natural self. The men I dated never saw the real me. They only saw what I wanted them to see. But come tomorrow morning, I would reveal my true self to Gabriel. Wouldn't he be surprised when he found out I wasn't his type at all? Long brown wavy hair and rich chocolate eyes. It didn't matter. He already hated me for what I'd done, and I hated him for locking me up in this room like a prisoner.

~

G abriel
    I tossed and turned all night, waiting for the pounding and screaming to start again, but it didn't. She kept quiet. I was worried. Would she do something stupid? Nah. She was too strong of a woman to do

that. She was plotting her escape. A woman like that wouldn't just sit back and take what I'd done to her lightly. I grabbed the key to the room off my nightstand and went to check on her. I needed to be careful because she could be hiding behind the door, waiting to hit me over the head with something and escape. We needed to talk.

After unlocking the door, I slowly opened it, stood in the doorway, and stared at the woman sound asleep in bed. I smiled at how her long blonde hair lay over her shoulders as she slept soundly on her side. The sad part was that she was beautiful no matter her hair color.

I turned around and headed downstairs, leaving the door open so she could come down when she woke up. She'd try to leave, but I secured the place, so leaving wasn't an option. I called Grace last night and told her not to come today. I first needed to assess this situation with Hannah, or whatever her name was. Walking into the kitchen, I grabbed some eggs and vegetables from the fridge and cut them up for an omelet. As I was chopping away, my phone rang. It was my secretary, Lu, calling.

"What's up, Lu?"

"Sorry to disturb you, Mr. Quinn, but you missed your meeting this morning."

"Shit. I forgot about it. Reschedule for another time, and I won't be in the office today. If anything comes up, have Thaddeus handle it."

"Yes, sir. Enjoy your day."

"Thanks, Lu, you too."

I returned to chopping the vegetables and heard a voice enter the kitchen.

"You do realize you left the door open, right?" she spoke.

"Yes. I know," I replied as I looked up and stared at the beautiful woman with the long blonde wavy hair and blue eyes staring back at me. I gulped as my eyes raked over her from head to toe. She was wearing a nightshirt. Short-sleeved, navy blue, and not long enough to cover her toned, sexy legs. "Have a seat."

"Why?" she asked as she stood there.

"Do you want breakfast or not?" I arched my brow.

"Coffee would be nice."

"The Keurig is right there, and the pods are next to it. Help yourself."

"And the cups?"

"In the cabinet above."

She walked over to the cabinet, made a cup of coffee, and began to walk out of the kitchen.

"Where do you think you're going?" I asked.

"Upstairs to the lovely room you provided for me last night. You know. The same one where you're holding me prisoner."

"I told you to sit down." I cracked the eggs in a bowl.

"I don't care what you told me. I don't want to sit anywhere near you."

She was testing me. Seeing how far she could push me, playing me.

"I said sit down!" I spoke in an authoritative tone. "We have some things to discuss."

"Like you letting me go home?"

"I'm afraid I can't do that just yet. Not until your debt to me is paid off."

"Are you fucking kidding me?" she snapped. "You can't hold me here against my will. In case you didn't know, Gabe, that's called kidnapping."

My blood started to boil when she once again called me

Gabe. I hated that name and wouldn't stand for her calling me that.

"It's Gabriel for the last time!" I shouted.

She snickered. "Someone has a deep-rooted issue."

I inhaled a sharp breath.

"The omelets are almost ready. Please sit down."

Chapter Nine

Kate

I was hungry, and his omelets smelled good, intensifying my belly growling. I sat at the table in the kitchen as he placed an omelet on my plate and set it down in front of me.

"What? No toast to go with this fine omelet?" I asked.

"Do you want toast?" He cocked his head at me.

"Yes." I smiled.

He huffed, took the bread from the cabinet, and placed it in the toaster on the white and black-specked granite countertop.

"What do you like on your toast?" he asked.

"Nutella."

He sighed. "I don't have any Nutella. What else?"

"I only like Nutella."

"Well, I'm sorry to disappoint you, sweetheart. I have peanut butter, jelly, or butter. Take your pick," he spoke in an irritated tone.

"Forget it. I don't want toast." I silently smiled to myself.

The toaster popped, and he took the two pieces out and threw them on my plate.

"Too bad. I already made it. Eat it dry, then. I really don't give a damn." He scowled.

He took his plate, sat across from me, and ate his omelet. Fuck, he was so sexy. It could be worse, right? One way or another, I was getting out of here today and leaving New York.

"So, Gabriel, do you have a last name?" I bravely asked.

"Do you have a first?" His brow raised at me.

"I have many first names." I smirked.

"No shit. Judging by all those passports, you must have what? Twenty or so?"

"About."

"Name?" he asked.

"What name do you want me to have?" I slyly smiled.

He slammed his fists down on the table, and I flinched.

"Damn it! Why can't you answer a simple question?" He got up from his seat and threw his plate in the sink.

He walked over to me, turned my chair around, and gripped my arms tightly with his hands, his face mere inches from mine.

"You want to play games. Fine. I'm in. This is how it's going to work. You stole thirty thousand dollars from me, and I want it back. Since you seem to con so many rich men, you must have a huge bank account or stashes of money hidden somewhere. Until I get paid, you don't leave this house. I have a high-tech security system, which will always remain on. If you even think about opening a door or a window, it will go off, and I'll be alerted. I have security in front of the house and the back. You try to step one foot out of this house, and they will stop you."

"First chance I get, I'm calling the police," I spoke.

"Go ahead. I have your briefcase full of your aliases and the keys to your apartment. I'm sure somewhere around this world you're wanted, and your ass will be going to jail for a very long time," he spoke deadpan.

"I don't have thirty thousand dollars." I looked away. "I can give you the ring Samuel gave me as partial payment."

"No. You're giving the ring back to him. You will not screw that poor man over. I'm sure he's devastated enough over the fact that he can't get hold of you. So you're going to write him a letter of apology and tell him you had to leave town, put the ring with the letter, and I will have someone deliver it to his office."

I couldn't help it. It was a gut reaction. I spit in his face. I hated people telling me what to do. I expected him to go into more of a rage, but he didn't. He grabbed the napkin off the table and wiped his face with it.

"Do that again, and you'll be sorry," he spoke calmly.

"Why is Samuel so important to you?" I asked.

"Because he's a friend, and I don't like people fucking with my friends. Now, I will get you a piece of paper and a pen, and you'll write that letter. Understand?"

"Computer," I spoke.

"What?" His eyes narrowed at me.

"No handwritten letter. It must be typed. He could have the handwriting analyzed, and it could come back to me."

"How?" he asked in confusion.

"I don't know. But I'm not taking any chances."

"Fine." He grabbed my arm and led me out of the kitchen.

"Let go of me."

"And take the chance of you running? No thanks."

"You already said I have no chance in hell of getting out of here, so where would I run to?"

He led me to his office and set me down in his high-back burgundy leather chair. Opening his laptop, he pulled up a Word document.

"Type."

"What the hell do you want me to say?" I asked.

"I don't know. You're the expert at lying. You can steal from people without them knowing, but you can't type a simple letter?" His brow arched.

Rolling my eyes, my fingers began clicking across the keyboard.

"There. Good enough for you?" I spoke with an attitude.

"Good enough." He hit the print button, and the letter spewed from his printer.

When he went to grab the paper, I stopped him.

"I wouldn't touch that if I were you."

"What? Why?"

"He could have it analyzed for fingerprints. And if he does, how would you explain your prints all over the paper? Common sense, Gabriel." I smiled.

"So, what the hell do I use?"

"Do you have a pair of gloves?"

"In the closet, I do."

"Then I suggest you get them, and we'll need to wipe the ring clean before you stick it in the envelope."

"Wait a minute. Wouldn't your fingerprints be all over his place?"

"Liquid adhesive bandage." I held up my hands to him and wiggled my fingers.

He took a deep breath, closed his laptop, and spoke, "Are you serious?"

"Yes. I'm very serious."

He slowly shook his head. "I'll be right back. Don't move."

Within seconds, he returned to his office with a pair of black leather gloves on his hands. He folded the letter, put the ring in a small plastic baggie, and retrieved a long envelope from his drawer. Pulling out his phone, he made a call.

"Carl, I need you to deliver something for me."

"Wait," I spoke.

"Hold on, Carl. What?" He looked at me.

"You need to put it in his home mailbox because he will interrogate every person in that building until he finds out who delivered it. If you use a delivery service, he'll contact them, and they'll describe you or whomever you send. It's too risky. But wait. He has security cameras inside and outside his house. He'll see you."

"Forget it, Carl." He sighed as he ended the call. "Now what?"

"Let me take it to a delivery service."

He laughed. "Hell no. Do you think I'm stupid? You aren't leaving this house, sweetheart."

"Fine. Then, mail it for overnight delivery, but type his address on a label. No handwriting."

His eyes narrowed at me. He was either delighted that I knew so much or disgusted. I couldn't really tell. As he prepared the label, I looked around his office. Pictures of him and his dad, I presumed, sat on a bookcase that was filled with books. On his desk sat a picture of him and a younger guy, someone who was as equally as handsome as he was.

"Who's this?" I asked as I picked up the picture.

"My brother, Caleb."

"He's cute. I bet he's a real lady's man like his brother." I smirked.

"Put it down."

When he moved me out of the way to open the top drawer of his desk, I caught a glimpse of something. A stack of Post-it notes that read: From the desk of Gabriel Quinn. How the hell did I know that name?

"Oh, my God. You're Gabriel Quinn of Quinn Hotels," I spoke.

"I wondered how long it would take you to figure that out."

"Yeah. I'll admit that I'm a bit disappointed in myself for not figuring it out sooner. Well, well," I leaned back in his chair, "Mr. Gabriel Quinn is a kidnapper."

"I'm no kidnapper. You stole something of mine, and I want it back. I'm simply keeping you around until that happens." He pointed at me. "I'm not taking the chance of you hopping on a plane to god knows where and me never seeing my watch or my thirty thousand dollars again."

"You have all the money in the world. Thirty thousand dollars is change to you." I rolled my eyes.

"Believe it or not, thirty thousand dollars is a lot to me, and when someone decides to steal something of mine, I don't take it very lightly. Let's go."

"Where?"

"Out of my office. In fact, you need to go back up to your room. I have to go out for a while."

"Seriously? You're going to keep me locked up in that small room while you're gone? There's nothing to do up there."

"Watch TV. It's the same thing you'd do if you were down here. Now let's go."

"But the kitchen is down here. What if I get hungry or thirsty?"

He took hold of my arm (I was really getting sick of him doing that) and led me to the kitchen. Opening the pantry, he grabbed a bag of chips and some almonds. Then he walked over to the refrigerator, grabbed two bottles of water and an apple, and handed them to me.

"There, you have your snacks and drink. You'll be fine until I return." He grabbed my arm again and took me up to my room.

"You know what? You're a real asshole, Gabriel Quinn!" I shouted as he shut and locked the door.

Chapter Ten

Gabriel

I sighed as I walked downstairs and headed out the door. Climbing into the limo, I dropped the envelope addressed to Samuel off at the post office and then headed to the office to pick up a file I needed so I could work from home.

"Mr. Quinn, I thought you weren't coming in today," Lu spoke as I walked past her desk.

"I'm only here to grab a file. Anything I should know about?"

She got up from her chair and followed me into my office.

"Your meeting from this morning has been rescheduled for Friday at nine o'clock, and Mr. Ingram called and needs to talk to you about the details of the hotel's grand opening in Hawaii."

"Thank you, Lu. I'll give him a call when I get home."

"Very well, Mr. Quinn. Enjoy the rest of your day," she spoke.

"You too." I gave her a small smile as I left my office.

Upon climbing into the limo, I pulled my phone from my pocket and called Grace.

"Hello," she answered.

"Grace, it's me. What are you doing right now?"

"Not much. Why?"

"Do you think you can meet me at Whole Foods?"

"Umm. Sure."

"Thanks. I need you to help me pick out something for dinner, and I need to discuss something with you."

"Okay. Are you cooking tonight? I can come by and cook dinner for you. It's no trouble."

"Thanks. I appreciate the offer, but I'm going to cook. Can you meet me in about fifteen minutes?"

"Sure. I'll see you soon."

Since I would be working from home, I figured I'd cook dinner for the girl who stole my Cartier watch and me. One thing was for sure. She would reveal her name tonight. Even if I had to fuck it out of her, I would know her real name.

Upon entering Whole Foods, I saw Grace standing in the produce section, looking at the peaches.

"Thanks for coming, Grace." I smiled as I kissed her cheek.

"You're welcome, Gabriel. So what special dinner are you cooking, and for whom are you cooking it?"

I sighed as I picked up a peach and examined it.

"I have a houseguest, and she'll be staying with me for quite a while."

"She? What's her name?"

"Well," I set the peach down, "when I first met her, she said her name was Hannah, but that has proven to be untrue. So, I don't know her real name yet, but I will find out tonight."

She narrowed her eyes at me as she began pushing the shopping cart.

"You're telling me that you met a woman named Hannah, but it turns out that's not her real name, yet she's your houseguest, and you still don't know her name?"

I placed my hands in my pants pockets and spoke, "Yep."

"What's going on, Gabriel?"

"She stole something from me and will stay at the house until she gives it back."

"I'm not sure I like the way you said that. Is she staying of her own free will?" She cocked her head.

"No. The first chance she gets, she's going to run. So, I need you to watch her while I'm at the office."

She stopped the cart and shot me a disapproving look.

"Gabriel, what did you do?"

"Don't look at me like that. She's a con artist. I'm doing the upper class a favor by keeping her at my house."

She rolled her eyes and pushed the cart over to the meat counter.

"I'm going to go out on a limb here and assume you had sex with her?"

"Yes. About a month ago."

"Before or after you broke up with Greta?"

"After. I met her on the plane back from Seattle. But enough with the details. Now, what should I make for dinner?"

"What does she like to eat?" she asked as her brow raised.

"I don't know. Does it matter? She'll eat whatever I make, and if she doesn't like it, then that's her problem."

"If it didn't matter, you would have come here by your-self and bought whatever you wanted. You wouldn't have asked for my help. My suggestion would be to get some salmon and a couple of steaks. She should like one or the other."

"Thanks, Grace. I owe you."

"You sure do, Gabriel. Especially if I'm now a babysitter." She smirked.

～

Kate

I lay on the bed, grabbed the remote, and started flipping through channels, praying and hoping something good would be on to keep me occupied. He could not, and I repeat, could not keep me locked up in this room. I'd go stir-crazy. Insane. How did he expect me to repay him for the watch when he wouldn't let me out of this damn room? I threw the remote down and began pacing back and forth, trying to figure out how to get myself out of this mess. I stopped and ran to the door when I heard footsteps in the hallway.

"If you're back, you can let me out of this room!" I shouted as I pounded on the door.

"Hello?" I heard a male voice that wasn't Gabriel's.

My heart started pounding. Someone else was here, and this was my chance to escape.

"Help me!" I pounded on the door. "Can you please let me out?"

"Who's in there?" the male voice spoke.

"Please just open the door!" I shouted.

"Lady, calm down. Why are you locked in there?" he asked as he jiggled the doorknob.

"Because the man of the house is holding me as his prisoner. Please help me!"

I heard him chuckle from the other side.

"Gabriel would never do that. Who are you?"

"Who are you?" I asked in a calm tone.

"Caleb. Gabriel's brother."

Ah, the cute one I saw in a frame on Gabriel's desk.

"Caleb, you have to help me. Your brother is crazy. He's holding me captive here in this room."

"I'm sorry, but I don't have a key. Where's Gabriel?" he asked.

"I don't know! He went out! Please help me. Can you find anything to open the door?"

"Umm. Like I said, I don't have the key. Just sit tight. I'm sure Gabriel will be home soon."

Was he serious? I began pounding harder on the door.

"Please, don't leave."

❧

Gabriel

As Carl helped me put the grocery bags in the back of the limo, my phone rang, and Caleb was calling.

"What's up, little brother?" I answered.

"I called your office, and Lu said you took the day off, so I came by your place. Want to tell me what's with all the security men outside and the woman that's locked inside your guest room? She said you're holding her as your prisoner. Do I even want to know what's going on?"

"I'm on my way home now. I'll explain when I get there."

"She was screaming at me to let her out and banging on the door. Bro, seriously, what the fuck is going on?"

I chuckled. "Like I said, I'll explain when I get home."

"When will you be home?" he asked.

"In about twenty minutes or so."

"And what do you want me to do? She's still screaming and pounding on the door."

"Ignore her. She'll eventually stop. I'll see you soon."

I took in a deep breath as I ended the call with Caleb. Shit. I didn't expect him to come over, and now I needed to explain to him what I'd done and why I was keeping her there. She had to talk to me and tell me about herself so I could figure out my next plan with her. But, as long as she remained tight-lipped about who she really was, she'd spend a lot of time in that bedroom.

As soon as Carl pulled up to the house, I grabbed the bags and entered through the service door to the kitchen. When I walked in, Caleb sat at the island eating a sandwich.

"Enjoying your lunch?" I smirked.

"Yeah, actually, I am. Grace can make one hell of a chicken salad."

"Did she quiet down?" I asked as I set the bags on the counter.

"Yes. Thank God. Now explain to me what the hell is going on."

"She's the woman who stole my watch."

"Shut up! How did you find her?" he asked as he cocked his head.

"I saw her at Samuel's Gala, except she looked totally different. Different hair and colored eyes."

"I thought you said she was only in New York for a couple of days."

"That's what she told me, which obviously a lie. She lives here in an apartment over on East 84th Street. She has a briefcase full of aliases. Different names, different looks."

"So you kidnapped her to get your watch back?" His brow arched.

"I didn't technically kidnap her. I tricked her into coming over, and now I won't let her leave until I get my thirty thousand dollars back."

"The price of the watch?" He narrowed his eye. "Where's the watch?"

"She sold it."

"Oh. Shit." He scratched his head. "So, she's a con artist, I take it?"

"Yep. She was conning Samuel Coldwater. He had given her a twenty-thousand-dollar ring from Tiffany. A ring that I made her give back to him."

"Ouch." He chuckled. "If she cons rich men, she must have the thirty grand to pay you."

"That's the thing. She said she doesn't, and that's all she'll say. I still don't know her real name."

"So, what are you going to do? You just can't keep her locked up in this house. The first chance she gets, she'll call the police, and then you'll go to jail. Do you know what that will do to the company?"

"She won't call the police. I have her briefcase with all her passports, different aliases, and the keys to her apartment. She'll be the one going to jail."

"Dude, I seriously can't believe this." He laughed. "Here I was coming to spend a little time with my brother, and I find out he's got some girl locked up in one of the guest rooms. I thought maybe you were doing something kinky." He smiled.

"I wish it was something like that. I guess I better go check on her."

As I began walking out of the kitchen, Caleb stopped me.

"Hey, Gabriel?"

"Yeah." I turned around.

"Remember when you first told me about the watch, and I told you I believed it just wasn't about that?"

"Yeah. I remember."

"I still think this isn't about the watch."

I looked away and headed up the stairs.

Chapter Eleven

Kate

I was sitting on the floor with my back against the door when I heard the key enter the lock. Standing up, I stood in front of it as he opened the door.

"Are you done screaming and pounding?" Gabriel asked.

"I am. For now, at least."

"Come downstairs and meet my brother Caleb."

"Why should I? Why would I want to meet a man who turned his back on me and refused to help?"

"There's nothing he could have done. He didn't have the key, and you can't unlock this type of lock with a credit card."

"Now I have to question what kind of person you really are." I arched my brow. "Who has locks like that on their bedroom doors?"

"To be honest, these locks were on the doors when I bought the house. I had found the keys tucked into a drawer in the kitchen."

"And you didn't think that was weird or bothered to have it changed?" I folded my arms and cocked my head.

"It wasn't a priority of mine. Please, come downstairs. I'll be cooking dinner for us soon."

Rolling my eyes, I followed him downstairs and into the kitchen where Caleb was sitting.

"Caleb, I want you to meet the woman who stole my watch. The woman who stole my watch, I would like you to meet my little brother Caleb."

"Nice to meet you. I think," he spoke as he held out his hand.

Placing my hand in his, I lightly shook it.

"I take it you aren't in the family business?" I asked.

"How can you tell that?" He cocked his head.

"By the way you look." I smiled. "You're more rugged than your brother." I took his hand and turned it over, slipping the watch off his wrist. "And you have calluses on your fingers. Are you a musician?"

"I am." He smiled. "How did you know?"

"I can read people very well." I smiled.

"I'm sure that comes in handy when you're ripping people off," Gabriel spoke.

I shot him a look and then turned my attention back to Caleb.

"Are you in a band?" I asked.

"I am. We're called Fallen Angels."

"Cool name." I grinned. "I play the guitar. Acoustic mostly."

"Really? How long have you been playing?"

"Since I was about eight years old."

"She's playing you, Caleb," Gabriel spoke.

"For your information, Mr. Quinn, I do play the guitar."

"Right, you do." Gabriel winked.

"Call her bluff, Gabriel," Caleb spoke. "You have that Gibson J-45 around here somewhere. Go get it, and let's see if she's telling the truth or lying."

Gabriel looked at me, his eyes burning through mine.

"Good idea, Caleb. I'll be right back."

Rolling my eyes, I walked into the living room and sat on the couch.

"Tell me how you did it," Caleb spoke.

"Did what?"

"Stole my brother's watch without him knowing."

"Why? Are you thinking of getting into the business?" I smirked.

"No. I'm just curious."

"I would show you, but I already took it." I smirked as I held up his watch.

"What the fuck! How?" He smiled in amazement.

Gabriel walked into the room and handed me his Gibson J-45 acoustic guitar.

"Here. If you can play, then play." His brow arched at me.

"I don't want to because I don't like your attitude, Mr. Quinn." I raised my brow as I set down the guitar.

"That's because you're lying. You told Caleb you knew how to play to make him believe you had a common interest, to gain his trust so you could play him."

"Whatever." I looked away.

"I'm going to start dinner. You can either help me, stay here, or return to your room. It's your choice."

"I'll stay here."

"Fine," he spoke with an attitude. "Caleb, come with me."

As soon as they left the room, I picked up the guitar. The feeling that overcame me every time I held one in my hands never got old. I placed my fingers on the strings and played A Thousand Years, singing the lyrics as I strummed each chord.

~

Gabriel

I set the knife down on the counter and looked at Caleb. Walking into the living room, I stood and stared at her while she played the guitar and sang. Her voice was beautiful and took my breath away. I swallowed hard, placed my hands in my pockets, and watched her. She wouldn't look at me. She just sat there staring out the window as she strummed each chord. When she finished, Caleb slowly clapped his hands.

"Wow. Just wow." He smiled.

She got up from the couch and handed me the guitar with sadness in her eyes.

"Thanks. I'm going to go upstairs for a while," she spoke.

"Fine. I'll call you when dinner is ready."

Caleb and I walked back into the kitchen when she left the room.

"Bro, did you hear that? I know you heard it. She's amazing, and she wasn't lying."

"I heard it," I spoke as I took the steaks out of their package.

"Listen, I have to go. The guys and I have practice. I'll call you later. Be gentle with her, Gabriel. There's more to her than just the woman who stole your watch. I felt and heard it in the way she sang and played the guitar. And I know you did too." He winked.

After I prepared dinner, I went upstairs to get her and

found she wasn't in her room. Shit. Where did she go? I knew she didn't leave the house, so I went up to the terrace and found her sitting on the couch with her knees up.

"There you are. Dinner's ready."

"It's nice up here," she softly spoke as she stared out into the city.

"Thank you. It's probably my favorite part of the house."

Since she liked it up here, I had an idea.

"Why don't we have dinner up here? I'll bring everything up."

"I'd like that." She gave me a small smile.

Placing my hands in my pockets, I began to head toward the elevator when I heard her call my name.

"Gabriel?"

"Yeah?" I stopped with my back turned to her.

"My name is Kate. Kate Harper."

A smile crossed my lips. Turning my head, our eyes met, and I gave her a slight nod before leaving the terrace.

Chapter Twelve

Kate

Telling Gabriel my name felt right. I'd never told anyone who I really was. If I wanted my freedom, I'd have to gain his trust, which I needed right now. But I'd have to be very careful because trust wasn't something he had of mine.

He rolled the serving cart onto the terrace and set the table for dinner. Walking over to the cocoa-brown wicker patio chair, I took a seat and placed a napkin in my lap.

"This looks really good. Thank you." I gave him a small smile.

"You're welcome," he replied, pouring some white wine into a glass and setting it beside my plate.

He took a seat across from me and picked up his fork.

"Who taught you how to cook?" I asked.

"My housekeeper, Grace. You'll be meeting her tomorrow."

"Can't wait," I spoke sarcastically as I sipped my wine.

"Do you have any family?" he asked.

"Yes, and I'm sure they're worried about me."

"Is there someone you'd like to call?" He pulled his phone from his pocket and held it in front of me. "I wouldn't want them to worry."

Shit. He knew I was lying.

"Go ahead. Call them."

I took the napkin and wiped my mouth as I looked down at my plate, breaking our eye contact.

"I'm going to assume you lied and you don't have anyone. The lies are going to stop, Kate. Do you understand me?" he commanded. "Are you even capable of not lying to someone? Or have you been doing it so long that you no longer know the difference between lies and the truth?"

"That is not true!" I slammed my fist on the table before getting up and walking to the railing.

"Then tell me one piece of truth about yourself!" he shouted.

"My name is Kate Harper. That's the truth. I'm twenty-four years old and have seen more shit in my life than someone my age should have. My mother died a day after giving birth to me, and my father raised me. We moved around from state to state, and I never had any friends. I couldn't get close enough to anybody because the minute I did, we'd move. Children grow up with best friends, Gabriel, but I've never had a best friend. I was too afraid to get close to anyone."

"Why?" he asked.

"Because I knew if I did, somehow or some way, something would happen, and I'd have to leave them. That was my life. That is my life."

"It doesn't have to be, Kate." He walked over to me and placed his hand on mine.

As much as the touch of his hand felt incredible, I couldn't allow it. Not yet.

"You don't understand, Gabriel."

"Then make me understand."

I took in a deep breath. "If you're going to keep me locked away here, then I will need some of my clothes from my apartment. Can you take me?"

The suspicious look in his eyes told me that the answer was no.

"I'm afraid I can't let you out of this house. You'll run, and I can't allow you to do that."

"Jesus Christ." I walked away, throwing my hands up in the air. "What are you, an FBI agent or something? Handcuff me, then. I don't care. You know my real name. If I run, you'll call the cops, and they'll track me down. I'm not stupid, Gabriel. I only want some clothes, so I don't have to keep wearing the same thing. Unless you want me to walk around naked?" I arched my brow.

"Fine," he spoke. "Go get your shoes, and I'll meet you downstairs."

"Thank you." I gave him a small smile.

I headed to my room, put on my shoes, went downstairs, and waited for him. I could do this. I could escape. I had one passport hidden under my mattress with about three thousand dollars in emergency cash. I heard his footsteps coming down the stairs, and when I turned and looked at him, he walked over to me and slapped a handcuff on my wrist.

"What the fuck, Gabriel?" I shouted as he slipped the other one on his wrist.

"You seriously didn't think I could trust you? Did you?" He smirked.

Well, there went my escape plan. I took in a deep breath to try and calm the anger that rose inside me. He led me outside, where two security men dressed in black stood guard at the front door, and Carl stood holding open the door to the limo.

"Watch your head," Gabriel spoke before I climbed inside.

"I'm not stupid," I sneered.

"I never said you were."

The ride to my apartment was silent until I had a question I needed answered.

"So, you just keep handcuffs lying around your house?"

"Yes." He smiled. "I keep them in my bedroom."

I narrowed my eye at him. "You're sick."

"Somehow, I don't believe you really think that. Are you seriously going to tell me that with all the guys you've been with, you have never been handcuffed during sex?"

"No. I haven't." I stared out the window, for I was telling the truth.

"Then I feel sorry for you. You're missing out. Maybe I can show you sometime how good they can be."

I tightened my legs at the thought. I could picture the whole scene in my head. Lying on my back with my hands cuffed together behind my head. His muscular body hovered over me, doing things to me that only he could. His tongue sliding over every inch of my bare skin, teasing me until I orgasmed. Shivers ran through me like a brisk wind on a winter day. I inhaled a sharp breath as I could feel the wetness form in my panties.

"Not going to happen," I spewed.

He chuckled as Carl pulled up to my apartment building. Gabriel climbed out first and carefully helped me from the car. Throwing his coat over our wrists, we entered my building and took the elevator up to my apartment.

"Can you at least un-cuff me so I can pack?" I asked.

"Hmm—No."

"Gabriel, come on!"

"I said no, Kate. You're staying cuffed. I don't trust you."

"And I don't trust you!" I shouted.

"Okay then. So we're just two people who don't trust each other. Now get packing so we can go home," he commanded.

"I am home, you idiot. Your place is far from home to me."

"I'm not discussing this any further. You can either pack your shit and return with me or go to jail. The choice is yours, sweetheart."

"What the fuck is the difference? Either place is jail!" I spoke with an attitude as I threw my suitcase on the bed.

I never should have fucked him. Okay, yes, I should have because he was sexy as sin, but I never should have taken his damn watch. How the hell did he know it was me? I'd done the test before, and none of the others knew I was the same person. I threw my things in the suitcase and shut it.

"Here. You can carry this. I have something else I need to grab," I spoke as I walked back into my closet and grabbed my guitar case, pulling Gabriel along with me.

We climbed back into the limo and drove back to his house. As I stared out the window silently, I felt the handcuff unlock. When I looked over at him, the corners of his mouth slightly curved upward.

"Thank you." I rubbed my sore wrist.

"You're welcome," he spoke as he uncuffed himself. "You can end all of this and go home."

"What are you talking about?"

"You say you don't have the money to repay me, but I know that's not true. You con people, Kate, for financial gain. Do you really expect me to believe you have no money?"

"Don't believe me. I don't care, Gabriel. I don't have thirty thousand dollars to give you."

"Then what the hell did you do with all the money you took?"

I took in a deep breath and stared out the window as we approached his house.

"I had things to pay off."

"What types of things? Or is it none of my business?"

"I can't talk about it right now. So please, just let it go. I'll figure out a way to get your money. I can do one last job, and then you'll never have to see me again."

We climbed out of the limo, and he lightly grabbed my arm.

"I will not take stolen money," he spoke in an irritated tone. "Go to your room. I'll bring your bag up later."

Grabbing my suitcase from him, I held it in one hand and my guitar case in the other.

"I can carry it up myself." I turned my head and headed towards the elevator.

Chapter Thirteen

Gabriel

Shaking my head, I walked over to the bar and poured myself a bourbon. It was late, and I was tired. She moved around a lot. But why? She said her father wasn't in the military, but that was all the information she offered. I felt she had to be secretive her whole life, and that was why she wouldn't tell me much about herself or her childhood. I needed to figure out what I would do with her and how I would get my money back. I still didn't believe she had no money, and judging by her apartment, she was paying a pretty penny.

I threw back the rest of my bourbon, headed upstairs to check on her, and locked the door before I went to bed. When I reached her room, I lightly knocked, and she told me to go away. Rolling my eyes, I opened it and found her lying across her bed on her stomach, propped up on her elbows and reading a magazine. She was in a purple satin two-piece short set, and she looked sexy as hell. Her long blonde hair was wrapped up with a clip in the back securing it. I took in a sharp breath as my cock started to rise.

"I didn't invite you in," she said as she turned the magazine page.

"It's my house. I don't need your permission to enter this room."

"What do you want, Gabriel?" Her piercing blue eyes looked up at me as she asked in irritation.

"I was just checking to see if you needed anything before I went to bed."

"I'm fine."

"Okay, then. Good night."

"Night."

I shut the door and stopped when I went to insert the key into the lock. Fuck it. She didn't need to be locked in there. She wouldn't get past the porch if she tried to escape tonight. So, I put the key in my pocket and headed to my room.

I awoke out of a sound sleep at one thirty a.m. My throat was dry, and when I reached for the bottle of water on the nightstand, I found it empty. Sighing, I climbed out of bed and headed to the kitchen.

"Can't sleep?" I asked Kate as she stood with the refrigerator door open.

She jumped.

"Shit, Gabriel. You scared me," she spoke as she placed her hand over her heart.

"Sorry. I just came down for a bottle of water."

"And I came down for some food. I'm hungry."

Seeing her standing there in her pajamas was wreaking havoc on my cock. All I could think about was how good it felt when I fucked her that day.

~

Kate

Looking at him, I caught his eyes raking over me from head to toe. I could tell he wanted to devour me. He stood there in his black pajama bottoms. His six-pack was shredded, chest puffed out, perfectly sculpted biceps, and the hint of a V-line that I found so incredibly attractive. I already knew what he sported underneath those pants, and as much as I hated him for what he was doing to me, I still wanted him inside me again.

He reached over to grab a bottle of water, lightly brushing his arm against my boob. I gulped. Our eyes met briefly, and then he turned and began to walk away.

"Gabriel?"

"Yeah."

"How did you know it was me?"

He set the water bottle on the counter and invaded the small space around me. Bringing his hand to my cheek, he said, "Your smile."

The serious look in his eyes sent me spiraling down a slope so fast I could barely catch my breath. I reached up and brushed my lips against his. He wrapped his arm around my waist and pulled me into him as our kiss deepened. My hands raked through his hair as his tongue slid across my neck, and I could feel the hardness of his cock as he pressed up against me. His fingers slipped around the thin straps of my pajama top, sliding them off my shoulders and letting it fall to the ground. His hands groped my breasts before moving down my torso and slipping down the front of my pajama shorts. A gasp escaped me when his fingers touched my most sensitive and aroused area. I heard the sharp inhale of his breath as he felt the wetness that escaped me.

"We have to go upstairs," he spoke with bated breath. "I don't have any condoms down here."

I couldn't wait until we got upstairs. I was so turned on and horny that it didn't matter to me whether he used a condom or not.

"I'm on birth control," I whispered.

His mouth smashed into mine as his finger dipped inside me. My knees went weak, causing me to lose balance. My entire body was engulfed in pleasure by the man who held me prisoner in his home. I'd already had him once, and I wanted him again.

He tightly gripped my ass with both hands and lifted me. Wrapping my legs around him, our lips tangled with pleasure as he carried me into the living room and laid me down on the floor in front of the fireplace. After he flipped the switch on the wall and the fire brightly started, he bent down, removed my shorts, and slid his tongue along my slick opening, causing me to cry out in ecstasy. The skillfulness of his tongue penetrated me in ways I'd never felt before, bringing me to the brink of an orgasm. My heart was racing, and my breath hitched as my legs tightened around his head, and I let out a howl as I came.

"Beautiful. Just beautiful." He smiled as he slipped off his pajama bottoms and hovered over me.

As amazing as that orgasm was, I knew the best was yet to come. His lips brushed against mine before traveling down to my breasts, where his mouth wrapped around my hardened nipple, and his tongue moved around it in circular motions. He took hold of my wrists and brought them over my head, interlocking them with one hand while he used the other to guide his cock inside me. The first thrust was slow and sensual as his eyes stared into mine. I took him in, his entire length, and gasped at the contentment that took over my body. He moved in and out of me with long, deep strokes as he held onto my wrists and his free hand groped my breast. His head dipped, and our lips met once again. After a few invigorating thrusts, he rolled over on his back and pulled me on top of him. My hands planted themselves firmly on his muscular chest as my hips moved back and forth, grinding against his hard cock, sending my body into overdrive. His arms clutched around my back as he sat up, forcing my legs to wrap around his waist. I slowly moved up and down and then back and forth as moans escaped our lips, tangled to the same rhythm of our movements.

"God, you feel amazing," Gabriel whispered.

"So do you. I'm going to come again," I panted.

"Try to hold off and wait for me. I'm close."

Moans escaped us while we moved together, bringing us to the heightened state we both desperately needed. I was there, my body was ready, and there was no holding back.

"Oh, God." I threw my head back as my legs tightened around his waist.

He held me down and moaned as he strained to push every drop of come he had inside me. Our bodies relaxed, and my head lay on his shoulder while our heart rates fell back into a normal range. The anger I had kept inside me for him started to dissipate. He broke our embrace and pushed my hair from my face, giving me a smile that sent shivers down my spine.

"We better get some sleep," he spoke.

"Yeah. I think we should."

"I'm not so sure sleeping in the same bed is a good idea."

"Probably not." My eyes stared into his.

I climbed off him, slipped into my pajama shorts, and retrieved my shirt in the kitchen. When I returned to the living room, Gabriel stood in his pajama bottoms with his arm held out. Placing mine in his, we headed up the numerous flights of stairs. He stopped on the fourth floor, and I continued up one more flight to my room.

I felt like I was in a daze and as if the world around me stood still, a feeling I'd only felt once in my entire life. That day at the airport when we were together. But I quickly let it go because I knew I'd never see him again. Now, I would see him every day, and I wasn't sure how I would be able to handle it. I was happy he wanted to sleep in separate rooms because if I was in his bed, wrapped around his sexy and warm body all night, I didn't think I would be able to go through with my plan. I needed to keep my emotions out of this and at a distance. It was something I had mastered a long time ago, but Gabriel was different from any other man I dated or had sex with, and it scared the shit out of me.

Chapter Fourteen

Gabriel

I climbed into bed, her smell lingering all over my body and her taste still on my lips. Rolling on my side, I stared at the empty spot where she should have been lying. But I couldn't allow it because if I did, I wasn't sure if I could let her go once all was said and done. I needed to remember what kind of person she was. Kate Harper conned rich men for their money. She used them, made them fall in love, and stole right out from under them.

The next morning, after showering and dressed for the office, I went downstairs to the kitchen, where Grace was preparing breakfast.

"Good morning, Gabriel." She smiled.

"Morning. Is she up yet?" I asked as I made a cup of coffee.

"Not that I know of. By the way, did you find out her name?"

"Her name is Kate Harper. I guess I better go check on her."

Taking my coffee with me, I took the elevator to the fifth floor, and when I lightly pushed the door open, I found her sound asleep in her bed. The corners of my mouth curved upward into a small smile as I leaned up against the doorway and stared at her. She looked like an angel, but an angel was something she was far from.

"She's still sleeping," I told Grace as I set my coffee cup on the counter. "I have to leave for the office now. If she gives you any trouble, call me immediately."

"I will. But I'm sure she won't be a problem."

I chuckled. "You haven't met her yet."

≈

Kate

I let out a long yawn as I stretched my body across the bed. I turned my head towards the window, taking note of the streaks of sunlight that cascaded through the sheer blinds. I climbed out of bed and hopped into the shower before heading downstairs for coffee. As I made my way into the kitchen, I noticed a shorter woman, about five foot four, with sandy brown hair that sat in a bun on top of her head, standing at the stove.

"You must be Grace," I spoke.

She turned around, stared at me briefly, and then smiled.

"You must be Kate." She held out her small, slender hand.

"Yes, and I'm sure Gabriel has told you all about me." I placed my hand in hers and lightly shook it.

"Just a bit. Would you like some coffee?"

"That would be great. Thank you," I spoke as I took a seat on the stool at the island.

"He told me that you stole something from him and you'd stay here until he got it back. May I ask what you took?"

"His Cartier watch."

"Oh." She bit her lip as she placed a cup of coffee in front of me.

"Is Gabriel here?" I asked.

"No. He's left for the office already. Can I make you some breakfast?"

"I can make it myself. I'm sure you have other things to do around this monstrous house."

"It's no trouble. Do you like French toast?" She smiled. "I have strawberries and whipped cream to put on top of it."

"That sounds really good." A grin crossed my face.

Grace seemed cool, and so far, I thought she didn't judge me for what I'd done. She appeared to be in her mid-fifties, wore no makeup, and had beautiful brown eyes.

"How long have you worked for Gabriel?" I asked as I took a sip of my coffee.

"A couple of years. I used to work for his father, and after he passed away, Gabriel hired me to work for him."

"Oh. So, you've known him for a long time?"

"Since he was ten years old." She smiled.

"Then you must know him well. Does he normally kidnap women and keep them hostage in his house?"

She let out a light laugh. "No, sweetie, you're the first."

"Aren't I the lucky one." I sipped my coffee.

"Gabriel tells me you're a con artist."

"I prefer the term 'entrepreneur.'" I smirked. "You don't by any chance have about thirty grand you can lend me so I can get out of here, do you?"

"I wish." She placed the French toast on a plate, topped it with strawberries and whipped cream, and set it down in front of me. "Gabriel is a good man, Kate, and he didn't deserve to be ripped off."

And here came the judging.

"If he's so great, why is he still single?" I arched my brow at her.

"He's a very busy man, and relationships aren't his top priority right now. He just ended a six-month relationship."

"Why?" I asked as I took a bite of my French toast.

"Greta wasn't the right girl for him."

"And who is the right girl for him?" I asked.

"Someone who is kind, truthful, selfless, and understanding of his work." Her brow raised in an accusatory way at me.

"Listen, Grace. You don't know anything about me or what I've been through, so stop with the judgy eyes."

"Everybody has been through something, Kate. So, stop playing the victim because the world dealt you a bad hand. What does your mother think? Or doesn't she know exactly what you do?"

Wow. Was this woman serious? Who the hell did she think she was talking to me like that?

"I don't and have never had a mother. She passed away the day after giving birth to me."

The judgment in her eyes dissipated as she stared at me.

"I'm sorry. What about your father?"

"He's not around." I looked down as I placed my fork on the plate.

"So, you're all alone?" she asked as she took my empty plate.

"Basically." I got up from my stool. "Thanks for the French toast," I said as I walked away before she had a chance to ask any more questions or felt the need to criticize me.

I distinctly remember Gabriel telling me at the airport that he was single. Did he lie? Did he just say that so I'd let him fuck me? If that was the case, he deserved to have his watch stolen. I needed to find out when he broke it off with that woman named Greta and why.

Chapter Fifteen

Gabriel

I was sitting behind my desk on a phone call when my brother Caleb popped his head through the door. Waving my hand, I motioned for him to come in.

"Thanks, Brian. My design team will be in touch."

I ended the call and leaned back in my chair.

"What's up, Caleb? You never drop by the office."

"I know, but I was just down the street having lunch, so I thought I'd drop in and see how things were going. Did you find out her name yet?" He smirked.

"Her name is Kate Harper and she's a twenty-four-year-old woman who was raised by her father."

"So does that mean Daddy also conned people?"

"I don't know. She won't talk about him. But she did say they moved around a lot, so I'm assuming he did."

"What are you going to do with her? You can't keep her locked up in your house."

I sighed. "I know. I was thinking about giving her a job here."

A light chuckle escaped him. "Seriously? Doing what? Listen, big brother, I know there's something inside you that feels like you need to save her. I just think it would be in your best interest to cut her loose. Forget about the watch and just move on. You don't need that kind of bullshit in your life. She's a con artist, bro. Once a con, always a con, and nothing you can do or say will ever change that."

Bringing my index fingers together, I brought them up to my lips. "I'm fully aware of that. But—"

"Oh, come on." He laughed. "Don't tell me you're in love with her?"

"I'm not in love with her. There's just something about her."

"I know that, Gabriel. I'm not stupid. I told you that it was about more than just the watch before. She's toxic, and you don't need that in your life. Isn't that why you got rid of Greta?"

"Greta was a child."

He pointed his finger at me. "I know what this is." He shook it. "This is about you being a rebel and doing something no one would ever expect from Gabriel Quinn. You spent your whole life doing what Dad wanted you to do. You never got in trouble, and you stayed on the path of his life. Now, this woman that is every kind of wrong enters your world, and it excites you."

"Maybe." I shrugged.

"Or it could be because she's not falling at your feet like ninety-nine percent of the women do. You see her as a challenge."

"Maybe." I smirked.

He sat across from me with a smile, shaking his head.

"I have to go." He got up from his chair. "We're playing

at the Crowfoot tonight if you want to come. And if you do, bring Kate along."

"Maybe." I gave him a small smile.

I spent the entire day thinking about Kate. It was crazy how much this woman was on my mind. Caleb was right. I did have some feelings for her. I knew deep down, and underneath the façade of her cons, a little girl was lost.

When five o'clock approached, and I'd finished signing the last of the contracts, I packed up my briefcase and headed home. When I walked through the door, Grace was putting on her coat.

"How did it go today?" I asked.

"Well, I made her French toast for breakfast, we spoke, and then she went back up to her room. That was the last I saw of her."

"She hasn't been down all day?" I asked.

"No, and to be honest, I preferred it. She has a little sassy mouth."

I chuckled. "I know she does. Have a good night. I'll see you tomorrow." I kissed her cheek.

Setting my briefcase down, I took the elevator up to the fifth floor and lightly knocked on the door to her room.

"Come in."

"How was your day?" I asked as I stood in the doorway.

"How do you think my day was, Gabriel?"

"If you chose to stay in your room all day, that was your problem. You had free roam of the entire house."

"What am I? A dog?" Her brow arched at me.

I couldn't help but smile at her sarcastic tone.

"Get changed. We're going out to dinner."

"You want to be seen in public with me?" she asked. "Aren't you taking a huge risk?"

"Just get changed and put on something nice. We're going to Daniel."

"What's wrong with this?" She pointed to her gray yoga pants and pink tank top.

"Kate, please just do as I ask." I sighed.

"I'm not going if you handcuff me."

"I promise I won't handcuff you. But if you decide later you would like to be handcuffed, perhaps to my bed, I will take great pleasure in fulfilling your wishes." I smirked.

"You're sick. Get out of here so I can change. I'll meet you downstairs." She threw a pillow at me.

I let out a light laugh as I shut the door, headed to my bedroom, and changed my clothes for dinner. As I waited for her to come down, I poured myself a bourbon and sat on the couch. A few moments later, I saw her walking down the stairs in a short, black, strapless dress and stiletto heels. Her hair was pinned up with strands of curls framing her face. She was stunning, and I couldn't take my eyes off her.

"What do you think?" She smiled as she did a twirl.

"You look beautiful." I grinned.

"More beautiful than Hannah?" Her cheeks blushed.

I walked over to her and placed my finger underneath her chin.

"Yes. You're more beautiful as Kate."

Kate
  I could feel the heat rise in my cheeks when he said that, and wetness flowed down below. Something about him made me tremble every time he looked at me. Maybe it was because he saw me as Kate, the real me. He held out his arm.

"Are you going to attempt to run?" he asked.

"No. That would be foolish of me since I'm starving." I smirked as I hooked my arm around his.

"Then let's go eat."

Gabriel ordered us a bottle of their finest champagne, and we started with a Maine lobster salad.

"Tell me about yourself, Gabriel," I spoke as I picked up my glass.

"What exactly do you want to know?"

"Anything. Tell me about your family."

"Well," he picked up his glass of champagne, "I was born and raised here in New York City. My father and mother never divorced but stayed unhappily married. You already know I have a brother, who is my only sibling, and I took over the family business when my father died two years ago."

"I'm sorry for your loss. If you don't mind me asking, how did he pass away?"

"Pancreatic cancer." He set down his drink. "It was very sudden and a complete shock to all of us. When he was diagnosed, he was already in stage 4 and passed away a couple of months later."

"That's awful. Were the two of you close?" I asked.

"We were. But not so much him and Caleb. My father wanted both sons to run the company, but Caleb didn't like the silver spoon he was born with."

"How so?" I cocked my head.

"He hates anything wealth, if that makes sense. He got kicked out of more prep schools than I could count and hung around with his own crowd. A crowd that my parents disapproved of."

"Why? Because they weren't rich enough?" I smirked.

"Pretty much. The only thing Caleb wanted to do was

play music. As soon as he graduated high school, he spent the summer in Los Angeles, and when he came back, he told my father he wasn't going to college and wanted nothing to do with Quinn Hotels."

"I'm sure your father loved that."

He sighed. "He kicked him out, took away his trust fund, and didn't speak to him for five years."

"And your mother?"

"She would try to get in contact with him, but he held her just as much responsible because she didn't try to make my father understand. Since the funeral, they've started reconnecting, but they have a long way to go."

"I can tell that the two of you are very close."

"We are. We always have been. Music is in his soul, and it's his passion. I never have, nor would I ever let anything come between us. My brother is my best friend, and I don't know what I'd do without him."

A small smile crossed my lips.

Chapter Sixteen

Kate

Listening to Gabriel talk about his brother made me envious. I had always wanted a sibling or a dog because then maybe my life wouldn't have been so lonely.

"Tell me more about you," he spoke.

"There's nothing more to tell."

"I don't believe you." His brow raised. "What about your business? Handbags, jewelry, shoes. All the things that make a girl feel pretty."

I bit down on my bottom lip as I stared at him.

"I don't want to discuss that," I spoke.

"Why? Because there is no business with handbags, jewelry, shoes, and everything that makes a girl feel pretty?"

"You know what my business is, Gabriel."

"Ah." He tilted his head back. "The men you con buy you handbags, jewelry, shoes, and everything that makes a girl feel pretty."

"Yes." I nodded.

He leaned across the table. "Tell me how you do it. How do you find these men?"

Before I could answer him, a shocked expression overtook his face as he stared over my shoulder.

"What's wrong?" I asked.

"Shit. Samuel Coldwater is walking this way. What if he recognizes you?"

"He won't."

"Fuck. We can't take that chance. We have to—"

"Gabriel, it's good to see you." Samuel smiled as he held out his hand.

"Samuel. Good to see you as well."

Samuel's eyes diverted to me. "And may I ask who this beautiful woman having dinner with you is?"

"This is Kate Harper. Kate, I would like you to meet Samuel Coldwater."

"It's a pleasure to make your acquaintance." I smiled as I spoke with a light Southern accent.

"The pleasure is all mine, dear."

"Are you here alone?" Gabriel asked him.

"I'm meeting a colleague for dinner. In fact, I see him right over there. It was good to see you, Gabriel, and a pleasure meeting you, Kate."

I smiled at him. He placed his hand on Gabriel's shoulder before walking away, and Gabriel sighed in relief.

"I told you he wouldn't recognize me."

"Let's get out of here," he spoke as he threw some cash for the bill on the table, and we left the restaurant.

As soon as we climbed into the limo, I turned to him and spoke, "He didn't look too broken up over Amy leaving him."

"He was there on business, so I'm sure he's camouflaging the pain he's feeling inside."

I rolled my eyes and looked out the window.

"You never answered my question," Gabriel spoke.

"What question was that?"

"How do you find the men you do to rip off?"

"Research. The internet is a powerful tool." I smirked.

"You're an incredibly intelligent woman, Kate. Why waste your intelligence by doing what you do?"

I turned away. I didn't like what I did. I hated it, but I had no choice.

"I'm not wasting my intelligence regardless of what you believe, Gabriel."

The limo pulled up to the curb of his townhome. When we entered the house, I froze when Gabriel asked about my father.

"Where is your father?"

I started walking up the stairs, ignoring his question because I didn't want to discuss him. The less he knew, the better for both of us.

"Answer me!" he spoke harshly as he lightly grabbed my arm.

"Let go of me!" I yelled.

"Not until you tell me about your father. Was he a con artist also? Is that why you moved around so much as a child? Did he teach you how to con people?"

I stared into his angry eyes. Why the fuck did he care so much? An uncontrollable movement happened as I smashed my mouth against his. His hand let go of my arm and wrapped around my waist, holding me steady and in place while our steamy kiss continued. In one swoop, he picked me up and carried me in his arms up five flights of stairs, our lips never leaving each other's.

He lay me down on my bed, hovering over me as he placed his hand up my dress, pushed my panties to the side, and plunged his finger inside me. I gasped as I tilted my head back, and his tongue swept over my neck. His lips, his hands, and his hard cock made me feel so good every time. Sex with him made me forget all the bad things that I'd done and all the people I'd used. With him, I was in the moment. With the others, I went to a faraway place. I was just me, Kate Harper, a girl born in Boise, Idaho. The girl I was before all the others.

His finger explored me while light moans escaped him as he felt the rush of wetness emerge from me.

"I'm going to keep doing this until you come," he whispered as his teeth nipped at my ear. "No matter how long it takes."

My heart rate accelerated faster, and it wasn't long before my body gave in and I orgasmed. Letting out a howl, my body shook as my legs tightened.

"That's it. Give me everything you have." His lips brushed against mine.

He climbed off the bed, bent down, pushed my dress up, slowly took off my panties, and began exploring me with his mouth, his tongue moving in circles around me. I gasped as I struggled to take a breath. I reached down and tangled my fingers through his hair while thrusting my hips up and down. After a few moments, he stood up and stripped out of his clothes while staring down at me. The look in his eyes was nothing short of hunger, and I could tell he wasn't going to be gentle with me.

He flipped me over, unzipped my dress, and pulled it off, tossing it over the bed and onto the floor. Hovering over me, his tongue slid up my back as his lips formed tiny kisses up to my shoulders. In one thrust, he was deep inside me. My hands grasped the sheets and clenched them tight as he moved in and out of me at a rapid pace. Groans rumbled in his chest as sounds of pleasure escaped my lips. His thrusts became faster as he sat up and dug his fingers into my ass while he pounded in and out of me. Another orgasm came, and his moans increased as he halted, pushing deep inside me and straining to release everything he had inside him.

He collapsed, his muscular chest resting upon my back and his arms wrapped around me. I could feel the rapid beat of his heart against me as I closed my eyes and took it all in. The safeness I felt was overwhelming, and I wanted to stay like that forever. Rolling off me, he stood up, and I turned on my back and stared at him. He grabbed his clothes from the floor, walked towards the door, and looked at me one last time before leaving the bedroom.

Chapter Seventeen

Gabriel

I put on a pair of sweatpants and a T-shirt and went up to the terrace. After pouring a glass of bourbon, I leaned against the cement rail and stared into the New York City night, trying to figure out what I would do with her. She conned rich men. She used them, and when she was done, she walked away with beautiful things and a lot of money. Money that she claimed she didn't have. I called bullshit on that one. She was a person I could never trust. I thought long and hard and finally came up with a plan. One she'd probably resist but didn't have a choice. Now, she was going to be the one to find out how it felt to be used, and in the end, she'd walk away with nothing.

After showering and getting ready for the office the following day, I headed to the kitchen.

"Good morning, Grace," I spoke.

"Good morning, Gabriel." She smiled. "Breakfast?"

"Sure. I have some time."

I walked over to the Keurig machine, popped in a K-cup, and heard someone stumble into the kitchen.

"Morning," Kate spoke as she sat down at the island.

"Good morning. Coffee?" I asked.

"Please."

As soon as my coffee was finished brewing, I picked up the cup and sat down at the table.

"What are you doing?" Kate asked.

"Drinking my coffee. Why?"

"You asked me if I wanted some, and I said 'please.'"

"And? Just because I asked you didn't mean I would make it."

Her eyes narrowed at me as she got up and walked over to the coffee maker.

"What am I supposed to do here all day?" she asked.

"I don't know. Figure it out."

"I'd like to paint, but I don't have any supplies."

I glanced up from my phone and looked at her.

"You like to paint?"

"Yes."

"Fine. Make a list of what you need, and I'll send someone to get it and have the supplies back here later today. And when I get home tonight, we're going to sit down and have a little chat. It's time you started paying off your debt."

"And how am I going to do that?" she asked as she sat at the table across from me.

"You'll find out later."

"Since we're both sitting here, you can tell me now," she spoke.

"I said we'll talk later," I firmly spoke. "Now, if you want those art supplies, you better start that list. I have to leave in a few minutes."

Grace walked over and handed her a piece of paper and a pen. I didn't know she liked to paint. But what did I really know about her anyway? She finished her list and handed it to me. After looking it over, I glanced up at her.

"Really? This is a lot of stuff."

She shrugged. "You can afford it. Or, I have most of it back at my apartment. Send one of your minions to go fetch it." Her brow raised.

"Where are they in your apartment?" I asked.

"In a chest in the corner of the living room. I'll need my easel also."

"I don't recall seeing an easel in your apartment."

"That's because you were too busy ransacking my room to notice anything else about my place."

"True." The corners of my mouth curved up into a sly smile.

I finished off my breakfast and got up from the table.

"I'm leaving now. I'll see you tonight."

"I'll be counting down the hours," she sarcastically spoke.

Grace let out a light laugh, and I narrowed my eye at her as I walked out the door. On the way to the office, I pulled my phone from my pocket and dialed Caleb.

"Hello."

"What are you doing for lunch?"

"Gee. I don't know. I haven't even had breakfast yet, bro."

"Can you meet me at the Shake Shack at one o'clock?"

"Sure. Good thing you picked that place because I wasn't about to go to any fancy restaurant with all that weird food."

I chuckled. "Why do you think I picked your favorite burger place? I'll see you later."

My meeting ended at twelve forty-five, and I had fifteen minutes to get over to the Shake Shack to meet Caleb.

"I'm heading to lunch, Lu. I'll be back in a couple of hours."

"Enjoy, Mr. Quinn." She smiled.

Carl dropped me off around the corner, and when I made my way to the restaurant, I saw Caleb standing outside.

"Hey." I smiled as we lightly hugged.

"What's with the lunch date?" he asked as we stepped inside.

"I figured out how Kate is going to pay me back."

Our order was up, so we took it to a table and sat down.

"Do tell, big brother," Caleb spoke.

As I told him my plan, he stared at me with a narrowed eye.

"I'm all for the first part, but I'm not so sure about the outcome."

"Why?" I asked.

"It's a little harsh, not to mention that I don't think you can do it."

"It won't be a problem."

"If you say so. Listen, Gabriel, Dad was always about teaching us lessons. You know that. This concerns me. You're playing with someone's life."

"Just like she's played with all those lives of all the men she ripped off. You think that's okay?"

"No. I don't. But do two wrongs make a right?" His brow raised.

"She ripped me off, and she will pay me back. Hopefully, she'll learn her lesson and not do it to anyone again."

"You know what they say: Once an alcoholic, always an alcoholic. I'm pretty sure that applies to con artists as well."

"We'll see, won't we? Anyway, what's going on with you?"

"I got a call yesterday from Atlantic Records. They loved the demo I sent them and want to hear more, so we're flying out to L.A. next week."

"Good." I nodded my head. "It's too bad things didn't work out with Sony."

He shrugged. "Everything happens for a reason, right?" He smiled as we both finished our burgers and got up from the table.

"You've always been the philosophical one in the family." I smirked as I placed my hand on his shoulder, and we walked out the door.

Chapter Eighteen

Kate

"It's about time, Carl," I spoke as he brought my art supplies into the house.

"Sorry, Miss Kate, but I also had other stops to make."

"Can you do me a favor and just take the easel up to the terrace?"

"Very well." He nodded.

"Thanks, Carl. You're a doll."

It bothered me all day as to what Gabriel wanted to talk about when he got home. He said it was time I started repaying him. But how? Was he going to give me a job at his office? That wouldn't be so bad. At least it would get me out of this damn house.

I took the elevator up to the terrace and moved my easel over by the railing where most of the sun hit and overlooked the city and river. This would be the perfect place to paint. I walked over to the bar area, took a glass, and filled it with water. Moving one of the small tables over by my easel, I set up my paint supplies, put a canvas up, and began painting. With each stroke of the brush, I was transported into another place—a place where I had no troubles or worries and a place where I could be me.

A few hours had passed when I heard the elevator doors open and Gabriel's voice.

"How was your day?" he asked.

"Fine," I spoke as I continued painting.

He walked over to where I was and stood behind me.

"You're painting the sea?" he asked.

"The sea is only part of it."

"It's beautiful. You have great artistic talent."

"Thank you. My mother was an artist. My dad told me she loved to paint and had a creative mind. She would tell stories with her portraits."

"And what's this story?" he asked.

"You'll see once it's finished." A small smile crossed my lips.

"I brought home dinner. Come and eat, and we can discuss some things."

"I'll be down in a minute. I just want to finish this last part."

"Very well." He turned and walked away.

Once I finished, I placed my brush in the water and took the elevator down to the kitchen. When I stepped out, I noticed Gabriel wasn't there, so I went to the dining room where he had the table set and bowls of pasta, salad, and bread were laid out.

"I got meat sauce, plain sauce, and Alfredo. I didn't know what you liked."

"All are fine. Thanks." I took a seat and placed the napkin on my lap.

My nerves were getting the best of me in anticipation of what he wanted to discuss, and I could no longer wait.

"So talk, Gabriel," I spoke as I picked up my fork.

He cleared his throat as he set his napkin on his lap.

"You're going to pay me back by being my companion for thirty days. A thousand dollars a night."

I arched my brow at him. "Excuse me?"

"You will work off your debt by having sex with me every night. You will do as I say and do what I want. You will attend events with me and travel if necessary."

"I'm not a fucking prostitute!" I deadpanned.

"Really, Kate? You seduce men, have sex with them, get them to fall in love with you, and then you take payment. If that isn't prostitution, I don't know what is."

"You son of a bitch." I shook my head.

"There's no need for name-calling. If you agree, which you really have no choice, you can leave the house, with a bodyguard, whenever you please. We will have dinner every night together, and then we will go to my room and have sex. When we finish, you will return to your room, and we'll see each other in the morning. Once the thirty days are up, you will leave and return to your apartment and your life."

"Are you so lonely of a man that you must resort to this?" I narrowed my eye at him.

"I'm not lonely at all. This actually works out perfectly for me. No emotions, no strings, nothing. And if you look at it, it's perfect for you too."

"How?" I asked.

"You're incapable of feelings. It's just another job for you. Clearly, you had no problems or trouble walking away from all the other men you ripped off, and I won't be any different."

"And if I don't agree?"

"Then I turn over all of your aliases to the police, and you go to jail."

"Ah, Gabriel Quinn, CEO of Quinn Hotels, kidnapper and blackmailer extraordinaire." I held up my glass of wine.

He picked up his and held it up in front of him.

"And Kate Harper, con artist and heartbreaker extraordinaire."

"You know nothing about me, Gabriel."

"I know enough. Honestly, I don't want to know anything else. Do we have a deal, or do I call the police?"

I couldn't believe his proposal. All this man wanted was sex. A thousand dollars a night of sex. If that was what it took to get me out of here, then fine. Besides, I liked having sex with him. This was my chance to play him, discover his weaknesses, and take advantage. He thought he was playing me, but he had just taken the game to a whole new level.

"I get to leave the house?" I asked.

"Yes. You can go wherever you want, but you will be guarded."

I rolled my eyes.

"And you said I would have to do anything you want in the bedroom?"

"Yes. Anything I want. You cannot say no."

I gulped.

"I don't do anal sex. That right there is out of the question. So, if you have the thought in that fucked up little head of yours, take it away now."

"If I'm paying a thousand dollars a night, you will do as I please, including anal sex."

I swallowed hard. He wouldn't do anal. He didn't seem like that type of guy. But then again, he did keep a pair of handcuffs in his bedroom. I'd call his bluff.

"Fine. We have a deal." I held out my hand. "But you do know I get my period. So then what?"

"We do it in the shower when that's going on."

"Okay. Thirty days it is, and then I leave. Can we count last night as day one?"

"No. It starts now, tonight. I do want to make one thing very clear to you. I am not like the other men you were with. I will not shower you with expensive gifts, flowers, or anything else."

"What if you're tempted to?" I smirked.

"Trust me, Kate. I won't be."

"Are you always this cold-hearted with the women you're with?"

"Only the ones who think it's okay to steal from me." He cocked his head.

"What about Greta?"

"How do you know about her?"

"Grace told me the other day you just ended a relationship with her. Why?"

"That's none of your business."

"Were you together when we fucked at JFK?"

"No, I wasn't. I don't cheat on the women I'm with."

I let out a light laugh. "Sure, you don't. You're a typical rich alpha male. Temptation is your weakest point."

"Not mine. When I'm with someone, I'm committed. I never once cheated on Greta."

My heart kind of melted when he said that, and I could tell he wasn't lying. He was faithful, a rare quality among men, especially men of his stature. But something different with him. He seemed cold and emotionless. More so now than before.

"Do you have any sexy lingerie?" he asked.

"Back at my apartment. Why?"

"Because I want you wearing it every night when you walk into my room."

"Then I guess we'll have to go to my place."

"No. I'll have new things delivered tomorrow."

"I thought you weren't going to lavish me with gifts?" I raised my brow.

"They're not for you, sweetheart. They're for me to enjoy."

"Seriously, Gabriel. What kind of freak are you?"

"How does me wanting to view you in sexy lingerie make me a freak? And don't even go there, Kate. I'm sure you've done some freaky shit with the men you've been with."

In reality, it was always just plain sex, very vanilla, which was fine with me. When the men would ask to try something different, I always told them I wasn't comfortable, so they would drop it and resume the regular plain and boring sex. Perhaps it was because I was never attracted to any of them, and I always had the upper hand. But with Gabriel, things were different. There was an enormous attraction to him, and I wasn't in control this time. Overall, his need for kinkiness turned me on.

"Do I at least get to pick out the lingerie?" I asked.

"No. Like I said, I'll have some things delivered tomorrow."

"And what about tonight?"

"For tonight, your naked body will do just fine. In fact," he looked at the time on his phone, "I want you naked and walking into my bedroom at nine p.m. Understand?" he spoke with seriousness.

"Yes, master. Anything you say."

He held up his finger. "Don't call me that."

The corners of my mouth curved up into a slight smile.

"What do you want me to call you? Daddy?"

"Absolutely not. What is wrong with you?"

Me? He wanted to know what was wrong with me. He was the one putting this plan of demand into motion.

"Fine. I understand, Gabriel."

"That's better. You have thirty minutes to prep yourself."

I got up from my seat and headed to my room. His plan wasn't so bad. Sex with him and the freedom to leave the house whenever I wanted was a pretty good deal, not to mention the traveling part. The one thing I did believe he was true to his word about was turning me over to the police. He had enough on me to put me away for a long time, and that wasn't something I was about to risk.

Chapter Nineteen

Kate

I looked at the clock on my nightstand. It was eight fifty-nine. It was time to make my grand entrance. I slipped off my robe and walked my naked body down to his bedroom. I had never been in there before, and I'd never seen it because he kept the door locked when he was gone.

He told me to come in when I lightly knocked on the door. Placing my hand on the handle, I opened it and stood in the doorway with my arm resting on the doorframe and my hip pushed out to the side.

"Come in," he spoke as he sat on the edge of the bed in nothing but a pair of pajama bottoms with his bare feet firmly planted on the floor.

I seductively walked towards him and stared into his hungry eyes. When I reached the bed, he planted his hands firmly on my hips, and his tongue stroked my belly. Instantly, the fire down below erupted, sending a tingling sensation through my body that made me tremble. He slid his tongue down to my clit, giving it a few strokes before circling my slick opening. My fingers raked through his hair as I closed my eyes, and pleasurable moans escaped my lips. His mouth devoured me while he dipped a finger inside, heightening my ecstasy. My breathing became rapid, as did my heart rate, and a rush of intoxicating warmth rushed through me.

He stood up and slowly circled around me, his lips barely touching my neck until he was fully behind me. He took my hand and placed it on his hard cock, moving my hand up and down the fabric of his pants. I tilted my head back, and his tongue explored my neck.

"It's time you got down on your knees and wrapped that beautiful mouth of yours around my hard cock," he whispered seductively in my ear.

Turning around, I brushed my lips against his before kneeling in front of him. Grabbing the sides of his waistband, I slid down his pajama bottoms and released his cock, which stood tall and proud. I wanted this to be a moment he'd remember forever, so I planted tiny kisses along his abdomen and up and down his sexy V-line before making my way down to his manhood. I circled his shaft lightly with my tongue while he gripped my hair and threw his head back, letting subtle moans escape him. Licking up and down, I stared up at him as our eyes met, and I could feel him tremble. My lips wrapped around him as I held the base of his cock with my hand, slowly moving it up and down while I devoured him. His moans heightened as his grip on my head tightened, and he thrust his hips back and forth. Bringing my other hand up to his balls, I lightly brushed my fingers across them.

"Stop. I'm about to come, and I don't want to yet," he spoke with bated breath.

He lifted me and threw me on the bed, bringing his lips

down to my breasts and taking my hardened peaks in his mouth. He grabbed my leg and held it up, thrusting inside me, forcing me to gasp for air. It was hard, deep, and full of promises to give me the ultimate orgasm. He pounded in and out of me rapidly as tiny beads of sweat formed on his skin. While I placed my hands firmly on his chest, he groped my breast with his other hand, giving each one equal attention. Sounds of gratification emerged from both of us as we fucked like a couple of rabbits, and I came.

He pulled out and flipped me on my side to enter me from behind. Another deep and hurried thrust jolted me, bringing me to the brink of another orgasm.

"Yes," he loudly voiced. "God, you feel so good. Fuck, Kate." He halted deep inside me.

When he finished, he pulled out and walked to the bathroom. After he returned, he handed me some tissues.

"You can clean yourself up and then go back to your room. I'll see you in the morning."

"Yeah, okay," I spoke with a hint of disappointment.

I got up from the bed and headed back to my room, my body still reeling from the effects of him. My mind was in shambles, and I couldn't figure out why. I felt used. Like I was nothing more than a piece of meat to him. I needed to paint, so I slipped on my robe and headed up to the terrace. The night was cool, but I didn't mind. Before starting, I walked over to the bar, poured a glass of white wine, and took it over to my easel while I stood and stared at what I had painted earlier in the day. Picking up my brush, I continued my journey.

$\approx$

G abriel

"Damn it," I spoke as I paced around the bedroom.

Trying to feel nothing for her at all was not easy. Sex was mind-blowing, and the way she had those beautiful lips wrapped around my cock, was amazing. Shit. It had to be this way. No feelings and no emotions. I needed to remember she stole my thirty-thousand-dollar watch right off my wrist without any guilt, and she conned many men. Watching her orgasm was satisfying. The look on her face and the way she lightly bit down on her bottom lip made it hard not to want to give her a hundred more.

I pulled on my pajama pants and went downstairs to my office to do some work. I wasn't tired, and I needed a drink. After pouring myself a bourbon, I sat at my computer and reviewed some emails. A couple of hours had passed, and I was finally tired, so I headed upstairs. I wondered if she was sleeping, so I went up to the fifth floor to check on her. The door was open, and her light was on, but she wasn't in there, so I went up to the terrace.

"Can't sleep?" I asked as I found her standing at her easel.

"I'm not really tired, and I wanted to paint," she spoke as she stared at the canvas and brushed a few strokes.

I walked over to her, amazed at how much she'd added since before dinner.

"A mermaid?" I asked as I stared at the painting.

"Yes. Don't you like mermaids?"

"I don't know. I never really thought about them. Is your painting telling a story?"

"Yeah. It sure is."

Her painting intrigued me. A beautiful mermaid with long blonde hair, sitting on a rock and looking out into the sea that was made up of blues and greens. I narrowed my eyes as I stared at it, wondering if somehow that was a depiction of Kate. As much as it intrigued me, it also confused me.

She set her brush in the water and gave me a small smile.

"I'm going to bed. I'll see you in the morning," she softly spoke.

"Good night, Kate."

I headed back to my room and climbed into bed. Grabbing my laptop, I opened it and googled "Mermaids." The description and symbolism I found validated my thoughts.

Along with unrivaled beauty, myth depicts mermaids with heart-stoppingly luscious voices. ... They are matrons of enchantment, entreating sailors with beguiling beauty, grace, and mesmerizing melodies. Seductive and charming, all those in contact with mermaids are subject to their persuasion.

The traits she possessed were the same. As beautiful as her painting was, it was also haunting. It almost felt as if she painted it out of pain. By the end of thirty days, I would know everything about her. I closed my eyes and tried to get some sleep, but I had a feeling sleep wouldn't be my friend tonight.

Chapter Twenty

Kate

I stretched my body as I opened my eyes and looked around the room. Since I was officially allowed to leave the house, I would take advantage of it today. I'd be gone the whole day. Doing what? Who the hell knew? I wondered which one of Gabriel's minions would get the luxury of guarding me. Would it be the cute buff guy with short blond hair and green eyes? Or would it be the bald guy who stood six foot four and looked like he hated life? He never cracked a smile and was always so serious.

Putting on my robe, I headed downstairs and went into the kitchen for some coffee. The closer I got, the more the aroma of something sweet captured my attention.

"Good morning, Grace." I smiled. "What is that wonderful smell?"

"Good morning, Kate. I'm making strawberry-stuffed cream cheese crepes. Would you like some? They're Gabriel's favorite."

"I would love some. Thank you."

I was happy today because I felt like I had some normalcy back in my life. I could come and go as I pleased and had to have sex with a hot and sexy billionaire. That was as normal as life could get for me. I would use my freedom to explore new options and make a plan for when the thirty days were up. I would be kind, sweet, and over-pleasing, just like I was with the others. I'd keep my feelings and emotions out of it. I had to. I wasn't a good person and didn't deserve to have someone as good as Gabriel. Not that he would want to settle down with someone like me. I had too much baggage, too much dishonesty, and too much of a screwed-up life for the likes of him.

"Are those strawberry crepes I smell?" Gabriel spoke as he walked into the kitchen.

"Yes, and they're ready. So go sit down," Grace replied.

"Good morning." I smiled as I walked up and kissed him on the cheek.

"Good morning." He narrowed his eye at me with suspicion.

I took my coffee to the table and sat down. He followed, taking the seat across from me.

"You seem to be in a rare mood this morning," he spoke.

"Maybe it had something to do with the events that occurred last night." I smirked.

Grace looked at me and then over at Gabriel as she set down our crepes in front of us. He didn't reply to my comment and began eating his breakfast.

"So, who's my babysitter today? Blond buff guy or the tall bald guy who hates life?"

"Huh?" Gabriel asked.

"I need to go out today, so which of your minions is tagging along?"

"And where do you need to go?"

"Out. I need to get out of this house. Walk the streets of Time Square, go to Central Park; hell, I'd even sit in a café all day to get out of here for a while."

"Edmond will be escorting you."

"And," I leaned closer, "which one is he?"

"According to you, 'tall bald guy who hates life.'"

I rolled my eyes. I had hoped he would say, 'blond, buff guy.' He seemed friendlier than Edmond.

"I have something for you," Gabriel spoke as he got up from the table and walked out of the kitchen.

A few moments later, he returned and set an iPhone down in front of me.

"I thought you should have this in case I need to get hold of you or you me."

"Thank you. But what about the phone I already have?"

"This one is special. The only number you can dial is mine." He smirked.

"Well, aren't you just a gem, wanting to keep me all to yourself." I smirked back.

"I don't trust you, Kate. You know that. You're only going to have it until our time is up. After that, you can have your other phone back."

"I don't need it anyway. It was only for Samuel. I always get rid of my phones after my job is done."

His eyebrow raised in dismay.

"I see."

"In fact, it's fine that I can only call you because who else do I have to call?" I looked away from him as I picked up my phone.

"Your father?"

I gave him a small smile as I got up from my chair.

"I would love to call him, but I can't."

"Why?"

"Because he's doing time at Rikers Island." I walked away and up to my room.

As I was in the closet picking out an outfit, I heard a light knock on the door.

"Come in."

"Your father is in prison?" Gabriel asked.

"Yes," I replied as I thumbed through my clothes.

"Why didn't you tell me?"

I shrugged. "I don't know. Maybe I was too embarrassed."

"So what made you tell me now?" He took a couple of steps closer.

"Why not? I mean, we're in this so-called thirty-day relationship. You might as well know about my family. Anyway, don't you have to get to the office?"

He stood and stared at me for a moment with a perplexed look.

"Yeah, I do. Enjoy your day out. I'll see you tonight. Maybe we'll go out."

"Really?" I smiled. "Where?"

"Caleb and his band are playing at the Bowery. I thought maybe we could go watch him."

"I'd like that."

"Okay, I'll let him know we'll be there." He smiled. "And by the way, we'll talk more about your father later."

"Gabriel?"

"Yes?" He turned and looked at me before walking out the door.

"I need my purse and wallet back if I'm going out."

"I'll go get it and leave it by the front door."

"Thanks."

After slipping on a pair of skinny jeans and an oversized grey sweater, I put on my shoes and walked out the front door. Instantly, Edmond stepped in front of me with a stern look in his eyes and his arms crossed.

"Relax, big boy. I'm sure Gabriel told you you'll tag along with me today." I smiled.

"He did."

"Great. Then why are you standing there like you're ready to wrestle me to the ground? Let's go."

~

G abriel
   Sitting behind my desk, I couldn't help but think about Kate's father. I knew something was up by the way she was vague about him. Rikers, eh? The apple sure didn't fall far from the tree, did it? I wondered what she was doing today. I told Edmond to keep a very close eye on her and his belongings at all times. Picking up my phone, I dialed Caleb.

"What's up, Gabriel?" he answered.

"What time are you playing tonight?"

"We hit the stage at nine o'clock," he replied. "Why? Are you thinking about coming?"

"Yes. I told Kate that we'd come to watch you play."

"Awesome. Come around eight, and we'll have a couple of drinks first. By the way, I take it she agreed to your plan?"

"She did because she knew she didn't have a choice. Which reminds me, I need to go. I have some shopping to do. I'll see you later, bro."

I ended the call, got up from my desk, and told Lu I'd return in an hour. Climbing into the limo, Carl drove me to Victoria's Secret, where I purchased lingerie and matching panties.

"Carl, after you drop me at the office, take this bag back

to my house and hand it to Grace. Tell her to put it on Kate's bed."

"Very well, sir." He nodded.

"You know what? Just drop me off at the deli down the street from my building. I'm going to grab a sandwich and walk to the office."

After grabbing a sandwich to go, I was walking down the street when I ran into Samuel Coldwater.

"Gabriel." He smiled as we both stopped on the sidewalk.

"Hello, Samuel. On your way to lunch?"

"I am. Care to join me? I was heading down to the deli for a quick sandwich. I have back-to-back meetings this afternoon."

I held up my bag. "Just came from there, but I'll join you."

I figured this was the perfect chance to find out about how he felt about Kate or, in his case, Amy disappearing. I wanted to know if he was looking for her. I grabbed us a small table while he went and ordered a sandwich.

"How's everything going?" I asked him as he took a seat across from me.

"Business-wise, things are good."

I narrowed my eyes at him. "Not so much personal-wise? Your gala was a huge success, and you have a beautiful girlfriend. Life should be grand, Samuel." I smirked.

"I'm not seeing Amy anymore, Gabriel."

"What? Why? The two of you seemed so happy."

"She left town the day after the gala and returned the ring I had given her."

"I'm sorry. I had no idea."

"How would you?" He gave a small smile.

"Did she give you a reason as to why she left?"

"She said she needed to go away to work on some issues she had with herself and be alone. If only she had talked to me, I could have helped. I was in love with her," he said with sadness.

I felt bad for the man.

"And you have no clue as to where she went?"

"No. A private investigator tried to track her down after I kept calling her cellphone, and it went straight to voice-mail, but no luck. He's convinced she wasn't who she said she was."

"Do you believe that?" I asked.

"I do. The more I thought about it, the more things didn't add up. I believe this woman was out to con me somehow."

"If she were, she wouldn't have given you back the ring," I spoke.

"I suppose that's true."

"Unfortunately, she was just a messed-up woman with a lot of issues. She did you a favor by leaving."

"Maybe you're right, Gabriel. Thank you, my friend. And you're right. She wouldn't have returned the ring."

"You're welcome." I smiled. "I need to get back to the office. It was good seeing you."

Chapter Twenty-One

K ate

I spent half the day in Central Park, walking around and taking in the beauty of the spring scenery. It felt good to get out of that house, and it gave me time to think about what I would do once my thirty days were up. My lease for the entire year had already been paid for, and my dad was here, so moving wasn't an option just yet. Plus, I needed a place for him to come to when I got him out of prison. Samuel Coldwater would have helped with that until Gabriel stepped in and ruined it for me. He was going to be my last con. The con that would help get my father out of prison and home with me where he belonged.

"Is there anywhere else you want to go before I take you home?" Edmond asked in a serious and monotone voice.

"Starbucks would be nice."

"Fine."

Rolling my eyes, I laid my head back against the seat and took in a deep breath. The thought of seeing Caleb and his band play tonight thrilled me. The less time I spent cooped up in that house, the better. Edmond parked around the corner from Starbucks, and we both climbed out and headed down the street, him walking behind me—something he'd done all day.

"You can walk next to me. I promise I won't bite," I spoke as I turned my head and looked at him.

His eye narrowed as he stared straight ahead. We stepped into Starbucks and waited in line.

"Coffee's on me today." I smiled at him. "What would you like?"

"Nothing." He stood tall with his hands folded in front of him.

"Oh, come on, Ed. Lighten up and have a coffee with me." I shoulder-bumped him.

"I'm fine, Miss Harper." He shot me a dirty look.

It was my turn to order, and the barista greeted me.

"Two Grande caramel macchiatos with non-fat milk, please."

"Name for the drinks, please," the barista spoke.

"Kate and Edmond." I smiled.

Hearing a heavy sigh escape Edmond's lips, I turned to him and spoke, "You'll love it. Trust me." I lightly hit his arm with the back of my hand. When our coffees were ready, I grabbed both cups from the counter and handed Edmond his.

"Thank you," he spoke as he cleared his throat.

A small smile crossed my lips. "You're welcome. Now let's go home."

Edmond pulled up to the curb of the townhouse, climbed out, and stood on the sidewalk, waiting for me to get out of the car. I sat there, staring straight ahead as I waited for him to open the door. His face twisted as his eyes narrowed at me through the window. Finally, he placed his hand on the handle and opened the door.

"Is there a problem?" he asked with irritation.

"No. I was waiting for you to be a gentleman and open the door for me." I arched my brow.

He took a sharp breath as he followed me up the steps, and I walked into the house. I noticed a Victoria's Secret bag on the bed when I reached my bedroom. Walking over to it, I removed the tissue paper and pulled out multiple pieces of pretty lingerie and matching panties. Gabriel had sexy taste, but I wasn't surprised by what a God he was in the bedroom.

Grabbing my macchiato from the nightstand where I had set it down, I walked downstairs to the kitchen to grab a small snack. As I passed the living room, I heard sobs coming from it. Stopping, I saw Grace sitting on the couch next to a woman crying her eyes out.

"Umm, hello?" I walked towards them.

Grace lightly shook her head at me as her eyes widened. It was as if she was telling me not to say anything.

"Who are you?" the woman next to Grace asked in a snotty tone.

"Kate. Kate Harper. And you may be?" I arched my brow at her.

"Greta Stevens." She sniffled.

Holy shit. It was the ex-girlfriend. What the hell was she doing here?

"Greta just stopped by to speak to Gabriel," Grace spoke.

This couldn't have worked out better if I had planned it myself. Sitting down on the couch, I hooked my arm around her.

"What are all the tears for?" I softly asked.

"A broken heart." She dabbed her eyes with a tissue.

"I've got this, Grace." I winked.

Her eye narrowed at me briefly before she got up and left the room.

"Are you his new girlfriend?" she scowled.

"Whose girlfriend?" I played dumb.

"Gabriel's."

"Oh no." I laughed. "I'm Gabriel's cousin. He was kind enough to let me stay here until my apartment renovations were complete. I just moved here from Texas."

"He never mentioned he had a cousin named Kate." She blew her nose.

"Well, maybe that's because he's an asshole." I smiled.

"But you just said he was kind."

"Yes. To let me stay here, but overall, he's an asshole. But you already know that since you're here crying on his couch. What did he do to you?" I gave her a light hug to play on her sympathy.

"Out of the clear blue, he broke up with me. And the worst part," she looked at me with mascara-stained eyes, "he did it over the phone while he was in Seattle. I can't seem to get over him."

"I'm not surprised." I shook my head. "How long were you dating?"

"Six months. He was the man of my dreams, and he did nothing but crush them." She laid her head on my shoulder.

"Ugh. I'm so sorry. Did he say why he broke things off?"

"He said he wasn't happy, and I couldn't understand that his career came first. He was always working. All I wanted was to spend time with him. Was that so much to ask?" She looked up at me.

"No, sweetie. Not at all."

"Then he told me I was a whiny little child and only cared about what I wanted."

"What a jerk."

"You know what the sad part is?" She lifted her head and blew her nose. "I would take him back in a second. Even though he shattered my heart into tiny pieces, I still love him."

This girl had some serious self-esteem issues.

"Do you really love him?" I asked.

"Of course I do. Why do you think I'm here? I was hoping to see him, and maybe we could talk."

"So, you were going to beg him to give you a second chance?"

She swallowed hard. "Yes."

I shook my head as I stood up from the couch and paced around the room.

"Greta, let me ask you something. Have you ever been with a wealthy man before Gabriel?"

"No."

"So when the two of you got together, you thought it was amazing that a man like him would fall for a girl like you?"

She looked at me with her sad, puppy-brown eyes. "How dare you."

"That wasn't an insult, darling. What I'm trying to say is that you never thought in a million years that a wealthy and sexy man would fall for you. Am I correct?"

"I guess."

"What type of men did you date before Gabriel?"

She shrugged. "Just typical guys. There was a construction worker, a paramedic, and a store manager."

"So just ordinary guys. Probably cute but not overly hot. Made an average salary. Perhaps enough to buy you a small house in the suburbs with a cute little white picket fence. Guys who worked nine to five and could spend all the time in the world with you? The type of man you only felt you deserved. Feel free to stop me if I'm wrong."

"So far, you're right." She nodded.

"Then along came Cousin Gabriel. Gorgeous, sexy, and rich. He made you feel like a million dollars when you only felt like you were worth a hundred. The thought that a man like him could fall for you was intoxicating. Finally, a man you could rub into your family and friends' faces to show them that Greta Stevens was someone special and that a man like Gabriel wanted her."

"What the hell is going on here?" Gabriel snapped as he walked into the room. "Greta, what are you doing here?"

I put my hand up to stop him from talking.

"It's clear you've broken this poor girl's heart with your ball-less way of breaking up with her. Over the phone, Gabriel? Really?" I narrowed my eyes at him.

"This is none of your business, Kate. Go upstairs!"

"Don't you dare talk to your cousin that way!" Greta snapped as she stood up from the couch.

"My what?" He shot me a look, and I smirked.

Walking over to Greta, I took hold of both her hands.

"Listen to me. You deserve so much better than him. You were in love with the fantasy, Greta. It was never really about Gabriel."

"It wasn't?"

"No, sweetie. No matter how poorly he treated you, you just wanted to hold on to that fantasy. You deserve someone who makes you a priority in their life. Someone capable of giving you all the love you deserve. Who puts you first before anything else. Gabriel is incapable of any of that, and you know it. He's greedy, and money is all he cares about.

Why do you think he's still single? Money will always be his number one love, and anyone else will always come second. Or hell, maybe even third. He has a heart of stone. But I know deep down you already knew that. Do you think that's something you deserve?"

"No." She lightly shook her head.

"Of course, you don't. From what I can see, you're a wonderful woman with so much going for you. You don't need a man like him. He can't be trusted, especially where women are concerned. He has a wandering eye, you know."

"Okay. That's enough!" he shouted.

"I know he does. I've seen it. The way he looked at other women when we were together."

"So, even though you were flying high with the fantasy, he was slowly making you feel inadequate?"

"Yes. As a matter of fact, he was."

"You're strong, Greta. Now go out into that world and show it how strong you really are and how no man will ever make you feel like that again."

"You're right." Her eyes diverted to him. "I never loved you, Gabriel. You were nothing but a fantasy to me. You, Mr. Gabriel Quinn, are mean, and you're a man who isn't capable of truly loving anyone but yourself. I deserve better than that. Good luck with the rest of your life." She grabbed her purse from the couch and walked past him. "I pity the next woman who falls for your dumb ass."

I snickered as she left.

"What the fuck was all that about?" he spoke angrily through gritted teeth.

"Relax. You should be thanking me. She came here to beg you to take her back. Did you really want to deal with all that nonsense?"

"Why the fuck would she do that?"

"Because, you idiot, she's still in love with you. It's beyond me why."

"She just said she wasn't."

"Because I convinced her she wasn't." The corners of my mouth curved up into a cunning smile.

"And all that shit you said about me is not true!"

"That has yet to be determined, Mr. Quinn." I winked. "It doesn't matter anyway. She's out of your life for good. Now, if you'll excuse me, I was on my way to the kitchen to grab a snack," I said as I walked away.

I went into the kitchen, and when I opened the refrigerator, I heard Gabriel's voice behind me.

"My cousin? Really?"

"Did you want me to tell her that you kidnapped me and are holding me hostage here as your sex slave for the next thirty days?"

"I did not kidnap you. You came here of your own free will."

"You tricked me." I pointed at him. "Isn't it funny how we all have a little bit of con in us?" I arched my brow.

He took in a sharp breath and placed his hands in his pockets.

Chapter Twenty-Two

Gabriel

I had no words for what I had just witnessed between Greta and Kate.

"You can thank me later in bed." She licked her lips as she walked past me.

My cock twitched something fierce, and it shouldn't have. Grace walked into the kitchen and looked at me.

"I'm all done for the day, Gabriel."

"Thank you, Grace. I'll see you tomorrow."

"I hate to admit it, but Kate sure is something else. Don't be too hard on her where Greta is concerned. She came here telling me that she couldn't live without you and that if you didn't take her back, she was afraid she would hurt herself. I tried talking to her and getting her out of here before you came home, but nothing worked. Then she started with her damn crying, and that's when Kate walked in. She has a way with words, Gabriel. You can't deny that." She smiled.

"She manipulates people, Grace."

She shrugged. "Well, in this case, it was a good thing."

I sighed as I went up to my room to change for dinner. Pulling my phone from my pocket, I sent a text message to Kate.

"We're leaving for dinner in approximately twenty minutes. Be ready. I want to eat before we head to the Bowery Room."

"Give me thirty. If you can't do that, then I will have to meet you at the restaurant."

"I said twenty or forget it. We aren't going out."

"And I said thirty. Do you really want to have to explain to Caleb that we couldn't come to see his band play over ten minutes?"

I clenched my fist and took in a deep breath. Throwing my phone on the bed, I took a quick shower and changed my clothes. I went downstairs and poured a bourbon while waiting for Miss Smarty Pants to come down. Looking at my watch, I saw that she had five minutes left.

"Don't worry. I'm five minutes early." She smiled as she walked down the stairs.

My eyes raked over her from head to toe as she took my breath away. She wore a high-waisted, pleated, short black skirt with a royal blue top that sat off both shoulders. Tall black boots that came over her knees graced her long, lean legs, and the way she had her hair pinned up with a few strands of curls hanging down started to give me an erection.

"Well?" She did a spin as she held out her hands. "Have I dressed appropriately for the evening?"

A smile crossed my lips. "You most definitely have. You look beautiful."

"Thank you, Gabriel. You look quite handsome yourself." She grinned.

As we were sitting in the limo on our way to the restaurant, I placed my hand on Kate's.

"I'm sorry about earlier with Greta. Thank you."

"You're welcome." She smiled. "I'm still trying to figure out what you saw in her."

"To be honest, I don't really know. I thought she was nice and sweet at first. But then, as the relationship grew, she demanded more of my time. Weekends weren't good enough. She wanted us to see each other every day, and she would cry non-stop. If I sent her flowers for a special occasion, she would whine that they weren't the right color. She would blow up my phone all day long, ask me what I was doing, and then Facetime me to make sure what I said was true. She nagged all the time. I took her on a business trip with me to Florida, and she only wanted to lie on the beach. And seriously, that's all she did the whole week we were there. She didn't want to sightsee or even shop. I was going to rent a boat for a day, and she claimed she got seasick, so that was out of the question."

"She sounds complicated."

"She was. She even had her mother call to tell me what a shitty boyfriend I was and that a man in my position should treat her like a queen."

"Wow. Really?" Her brow raised.

"It just wasn't a good thing."

"Then why did you stay with her for six months?"

"I was in the middle of opening a new hotel, and there were tons of problems. It was easier to stay with her and keep blowing her off until the hotel opened. Then, when I was in Seattle, she accused me of cheating on her and called me, crying her eyes out every day. I couldn't take it anymore, so I ended it over the phone. I didn't want to deal with her when I got back."

"She sounds like a psycho."

I sighed. "She pretty much was. Women don't understand that my career will always come first."

"I totally get that because mine does, too." She smirked.

"Very funny, Kate."

Carl pulled up to Tavern on the Green, and I climbed out first. Holding out my hand, she placed hers in mine as I helped her from the car.

"Tell me more about your father," I said as we sipped wine.

"Can we talk about him later? I just want to enjoy this evening."

"Fine. But we will discuss it."

After we finished eating, we headed to the Bowery Room.

"You made it." Caleb smiled as we lightly hugged.

"Of course. I told you we would."

"Hey, Kate. How are you?" Caleb asked.

"I'm good. Thanks. I'm really excited to hear you guys play."

"Thanks. Let's grab a drink before I go on stage."

The three of us sat at a table in front of where Caleb would perform. The place was getting crowded, but that was no surprise. Fallen Angels could always pack a room.

"Would you like another tequila?" I asked Kate.

"Yes, and don't forget the splash of lime." She smiled.

I headed to the bar just as Caleb and his band started to perform. When I returned to the table, Kate was in her seat, moving to the music.

"Wow. They're really good!" she exclaimed.

I smiled at her as I set her drink down. She sat and watched them play while I sat and watched her. She was having a good time, and I couldn't wait to get home and fuck her. The thought made my cock twitch. She was one of the most beautiful women I ever saw. Too bad she was every kind of wrong.

"Thank you all for coming out tonight to see us play. It means a lot," Caleb spoke to the audience. "I'd like to introduce you to someone. Her name is Kate, and she has the voice of an angel. Kate, come up here and sing a little something for us."

Kate was horrified, and Caleb wouldn't let it go. He jumped down from the stage and grabbed her hand, pulling her up with him. She tried to tell him no, but he wasn't taking no for an answer. He handed her his guitar, and she whispered something in his ear. Turning to the microphone, she spoke to the audience.

"This is a song my father used to sing to me."

I sat and watched her, listening carefully to the words as she sang them. The way she sang it was haunting. I could feel the emotion pour from her, which told me that song had a special meaning. When the song was over, the audience clapped and cheered. Caleb kissed her on the cheek, and she stepped off the stage. When she sat down, she finished her drink and asked for another.

"You were really good up there," I spoke.

"Thanks. I'm going to kill your brother for doing that."

The waitress brought over another round of drinks, and Kate chugged it as if it was water.

"Slow down there." I smiled. "That song you sang. You said your father used to sing it to you?"

"Yeah." She held up her finger to grab the waitress' attention. "He used to sing it to me all the time."

"What's the name of the song?" I asked.

"'Run' by Snow Patrol. The funny thing is that song fits our life so perfectly. It was as if it was written for us."

I sipped my bourbon while staring at her as she sipped her drink and watched Caleb's band on stage. She didn't say much the rest of the evening or on the way home, and I could tell something was bothering her.

"I'm going to go upstairs and change. Any specific lingerie you want me to wear tonight?" she asked.

"It's your choice. I'll meet you in my room when you're ready."

She gave me a small smile as we stepped onto the elevator.

Chapter Twenty-Three

K ate

I decided to slip into a black halter baby doll piece with the matching v-string panty. Walking into the bathroom, I took my hair down and ran my fingers through it, letting it fall over my shoulders. A sadness I'd been holding back all night pushed through all my strength and finally broke me. I sat on the edge of the bed with my face in my hands.

"Kate? Are you okay?" I heard Gabriel ask softly as he stepped into my bedroom.

I opened my eyes and looked up at him.

"My dad would always say, 'It's okay, Katie. Remember, we're on an adventure. Just you and me. Father and daughter. We can conquer the world together and do anything we want.' Except his conquering the world left me alone a majority of the time. He used to say, 'Light up, baby girl. One day, we'll have the life we always dreamed of.' He didn't understand that I wanted a normal life, with a house, and to stay in one place where I could set down roots and make some friends. Where he had a normal job and made an honest living."

He walked over to the bed when he saw the tears fall from my eyes and sat down next to me.

"He conned people, didn't he?" I asked.

I nodded my head and grabbed a tissue from the nightstand.

"Is that why he's in prison?"

"He got involved with some high-powered people. When they found out he conned them, they set him up and made sure he went to prison. The FBI seized all his funds, and he lost everything. A couple of days after he was sentenced to Rikers, a man knocked on the door of the hotel room I was staying in and told me that if I wanted to get my father out of prison, all I would have to do was pay them double of what he stole."

"How much?" he asked.

"Ten million dollars."

"For fuck's sake, Kate." He shook his head.

"They said once his debt is paid off, they would make sure he was released from prison."

"And they can just do that?"

"These people have friends in high places, Gabriel. You wanted to know why I do what I do. That's the reason. I don't like it. In fact, I hate it, but I need my father out of prison. He's the only person I have in this world." A tear fell from my eye. "I sold every piece of jewelry, designer clothes, handbags, and anything else those men gave me of great value. And whatever I take from them, I pay it towards my father's debt. That's why I don't have thirty thousand dollars to give you."

"How much of that debt did you already pay off?"

"Five million dollars. Samuel Coldwater was going to be my last job."

"How certain are you that these people would get your father out of prison after you paid them? People like that never keep their word."

"We signed a contract. I agreed to pay ten million dollars, and they agreed to get him out of prison."

"I see."

He got up from the bed and paced around the room.

"He ruined your life, Kate. You have to know that."

"He did what he had to do to support us. He told me I was the only thing he'd done right in his life. He quit conning after he met my mother, and they got married. He sold used cars, and they still had trouble making ends meet. Then I was born, she died, and I was all he had left. In his mind, he was doing what was best for us and doing the only thing he knew how."

Gabriel sat down on the bed and cupped his hands in his face. There were a few moments of silence, and then he stood up.

"Get some rest. Tonight is off."

I quickly grabbed hold of his hand before he could walk away.

"No. Please. I need you."

He turned and looked at me for a moment with hesitation in his eyes. Then he got down on his knees in front of me and brushed his lips against mine.

G

abriel

After I fucked her, I walked out of the bedroom and headed downstairs to the bar, where I poured myself a bourbon. She was upset, and I probably shouldn't have slept with her, but she wanted it. Maybe I should have stayed with her, but I couldn't. Her story. Was it true? Or was it all a lie? She was good at what she did, and I couldn't tell if she was playing me or not, which was infuriating. I threw back the rest of my bourbon and slammed the glass down on the bar. What was she up to? Was she telling me that story to make me feel sorry for her? To try and understand why she did what she did? Was she trying to con me into giving her money? Perhaps she was using me to get what she needed to pay off her father's debt. I wasn't buying the debt part. She did what she did because it was all she knew. It was how she grew up. She never had any structure and was never taught right from wrong.

The next morning, I grabbed a cup of coffee to go and headed straight to the office. I didn't want to be home when she woke up. I couldn't even look at her after what she had told me last night. As I took a seat behind my desk, Thaddeus walked in.

"I need you to review and sign these contracts for the Chicago property. Once that's done, we can start construction," he spoke.

"Hand them over." I held out my hand.

"Everything okay?" he asked as he sat across from me.

"Everything's fine. Why?" I looked at him.

"You seem unusually tense this morning."

"It's nothing. I just had a rough night."

"Greta's not back in the picture. Is she?" he asked.

"No," I replied as I signed the contracts and handed

135

them over. "Are we all set for Hawaii? Is there anything I need to know about before I get there?"

"No. Everything is smoothed out, and the grand opening is set."

"Good. I expect there to be no problems." I arched my brow.

"There won't be. I'll talk to you later."

I heard him say hello to someone as he walked out of my office. When I looked up, Kate was standing in the doorway.

"What are you doing here?"

"I was out and about and wanted to see where the great Gabriel Quinn spends most of his day." She smiled. "May I come in?"

"I'm really busy right now, Kate." I looked at my watch. "It's only ten o'clock. How are you out and about already?"

"This was my first stop."

"Where's Edmond?"

"He's behind me. I'm sorry to have bothered you. I'll see you later."

I called her name as she turned away and began closing the door.

"Kate."

She turned and looked at me.

"We're leaving for Hawaii in a couple of days. Make sure you start packing."

"And you're just telling me this now?"

"I was going to tell you tonight."

"And what's in Hawaii?" she asked.

"The grand opening of my new hotel."

"Okay. I'll start packing." She turned away and shut the door behind her.

I picked up a pen and threw it across my desk as I stood from my chair and paced around the room. I had this rage built up inside me that I couldn't let go of. It wasn't about the watch anymore. It wasn't being able to believe a word she said. I wanted to trust her, and I wanted to believe her because these fucking feelings that stirred inside me wouldn't stop.

After a long day, I could finally leave the office and head home. When I walked through the door, the aroma of something cooking hit me. Following the scent to the kitchen, I found Kate at the stove.

"What are you doing?" I asked as I set my briefcase down.

"Making dinner for us."

"Where's Grace?"

"She was finished, and she left. I thought it would be nice if I cooked tonight." She turned her head, and a small smile crossed her lips.

"I didn't know you could cook."

"Who do you think did all the cooking for my dad and me? If he had his way, we'd have pizza and fast food every night."

"It smells good. What are you making?" I asked as I took a seat at the island.

"Bruschetta chicken with a salad and homemade rolls."

"Did you teach yourself to cook?"

"Somewhat, and I had some teachers along the way. There was this woman my dad was with for a short period. She was a chef and owned her own restaurant. I spent a lot of time at her house, and she taught me a few things."

"A woman that your father conned?" I asked.

She swallowed hard. "Yes."

She took the chicken out of the pan, arranged it nicely on a platter, and took it into the dining room. Before taking a seat, I walked over to the bar and poured a glass of bourbon for me and a glass of white wine for her.

"This looks delicious. Thank you."

"You're welcome." She took a sip of her wine.

"What did you do today besides grocery shop?" I asked.

"Shopped a little bit for Hawaii."

"With what money?" My eyes narrowed.

"Who said I needed money?" A smirk crossed her face.

My blood started to boil at the thought that she had stolen the merchandise.

"I swear to God, Kate. If you—"

"Relax, Gabriel. I was kidding. I do have some money in my bank account. And before you ask how much, it's not thirty thousand dollars. Besides, I don't shoplift. I never have, and I never will."

I reached across the table and grabbed the salad bowl. As I placed some salad on my plate, she threw a roll at me, hitting me square in the face.

"What the fuck?!" I glared at her.

"I want to know why you have an attitude with me. I noticed it this morning at your office."

"I don't. Now drop it and finish eating," I sternly spoke.

"You do, and I want to know why. What did I do to make you so angry? I haven't got a clue unless you're still holding a grudge about your watch. But I thought we settled that. Isn't that why I'm here? I've done everything you asked of me so far. So there is no reason for you to treat me as you did or how you are."

Her mouth. She kept rambling, and it was pissing me off. I slammed my fists down on the table and stood up from my seat.

"You want to know why I'm so angry? It's because I can't trust you. I can't trust a word you say. That little fabricated story of yours last night was a good one. But not good enough for me to believe you or your lies." I pointed my finger at her.

She sat there as she dropped her fork onto her plate and stared at me, her eyes filled with tears. She slowly got up from her seat, wiped her mouth with a napkin, and set it on the table.

"I'm sorry you don't believe me. But it's all true. Everything I told you last night was the truth. I'm dealing with dangerous men, Gabriel. They want their money, and I want my father out of prison." She walked away and headed upstairs.

Chapter Twenty-Four

Kate

I ran to my room, slammed the door, and threw myself on the bed. Did I really blame him for not trusting me? Did I have the right to be so upset over it? Why did I even care if he trusted me or not? That was the big question. I needed to accept the fact that he would never trust me after everything I'd done. The sooner I did that, the easier this arrangement would be.

The only reason I was here was to pay off a debt, nothing else. He only saw me as a business deal, so the less I told him about my life, the better off I'd be. I was stupid for wanting to see where he worked and for caring that he left the house before I woke up. When I found out he was already gone, a part of me was sad, and all I wanted to do was see him before I started my day. These feelings and emotions were out of control, and I needed them to stop. I'd never had problems like this with the other men I was with. I never got involved and never felt a thing. I didn't even have to pretend, but with Gabriel, I did.

I refused to wallow in self-pity, so I got up from the bed,

took in a deep breath, and walked back downstairs to clean up dinner. When I reached the kitchen, I saw Gabriel loading the dishwasher.

"I'll take care of that," I spoke as I grabbed the pan from the stove.

"I've got it," he snapped.

"You've worked all day. Go upstairs. I'll finish cleaning up and meet you in your bedroom."

"Fine." He wiped his hands on a towel and began to walk out of the kitchen.

Before I knew it, he grabbed my arm, turned me around, and smashed his mouth into mine. Our heated kiss told me we wouldn't make it to the bedroom. My fingers fumbled with his belt as I undid it and unzipped his pants while his hands pulled my shirt over my head. We moved around until he had me pinned up against the refrigerator, the coldness of the stainless steel sending a jolt through me. He took down my pants, grabbed my wrists, and held them together with one hand while his free hand explored my aroused area. When he made sure I was wet enough for him, he pulled his hard cock from his underwear and shoved it deep inside me, causing me to gasp at both pleasure and pain. He moved rapidly, like a dog in heat, and his tongue slid across my neck. As he thrust in and out of me with hard, deep strokes, he stared into my eyes and spoke, "I want to trust you."

"You can," I breathlessly spoke as an orgasm erupted.

He halted and buried himself deep inside me while he came. His head dropped to my shoulder.

"No, I can't," he whispered.

He removed himself from me, tucked his cock back in his underwear, pulled up his pants, and walked away. I crossed my arms over my chest and slowly slid down to the floor, trying to hold back the tears that so badly wanted to stream down my face.

The next morning, after a restless night of sleep, I waited in bed until I was sure that Gabriel had left for the office. I had a lot to do today to prepare for Hawaii, but one thing took precedence: visiting my father. After showering and getting dressed, I headed to the kitchen, made a cup of coffee, and grabbed some fresh fruit from the refrigerator.

"Good morning, Kate," Grace spoke. "I can make you some breakfast."

"Morning, Grace. Fruit is fine. I'm not really hungry."

"You're up kind of late this morning. Is everything okay?" she asked.

"Yeah. I just had a restless night, and I couldn't really sleep. I'm going out today. Do you need me to pick you up anything?" I asked her.

"That's sweet of you to ask, but I have to go out myself and do some grocery shopping. Is there anything I can get you?"

"No thanks." I gave her a small smile as I sipped my coffee.

Grace left, and once I finished my fruit, I grabbed my purse and headed out the front door.

"Going out again?" Edmond raised his brow.

Usually, I'd have a witty comeback for him, but today, I was serious. To be honest, I think he was disappointed. I was making headway with him, and I started to believe he enjoyed my company.

"I need to go to Rikers Island to visit my father today."

"Oh. Okay. When are visiting hours?"

"Soon," I replied.

"Then we better head out now. There's going to be a lot of traffic."

We walked down the steps together, and he opened the car door for me. He was definitely making progress.

"Can you do me a favor, Edmond?"

"It depends." He looked at me through the rearview mirror.

"Please don't tell Gabriel that I went there today. I need it to stay between us," I spoke with sadness.

"Sure. I won't tell him."

When we arrived at the prison, I signed in, got searched, and then sat at an empty table while I waited for them to bring my father in.

"There's my baby girl." He smiled as I stood up, and we briefly hugged.

"Hi, Daddy."

"How are you? I haven't seen you in a month, Kate. I was starting to get worried."

"I'm sorry. Things have been so crazy. I have some wonderful news. I moved to New York."

"What?" He cocked his head. "What about your job and school in Chicago?"

"I got transferred here. The restaurant I work for opened up a location in Manhattan, and I asked if I could transfer to be closer to you."

"That's wonderful. But what about school?"

"I stopped going. It was taking me forever since I could only take a class here and there. But don't worry, I have a great job that pays well. Especially the tips."

"Are you okay, sweetheart?" he asked with concern.

"I'm fine. I have this great apartment in a nice neighborhood and have already made friends. The best part is, I can visit you every week." I brightly smiled to mask the pain inside me.

"What about that guy you were seeing in Chicago? What was his name? Tom, I believe?"

"I ended that a while ago. Things weren't working out."

"I'm sorry to hear that, sweetheart."

"Don't be, Daddy. It was for the best. Right now, I'm just focusing on myself and my career in the restaurant business. I'm learning everything I can because, one day, I would like to open up my own restaurant." I smiled.

"I'm so proud of you." He grinned. "I worry about you, baby. I worry about how growing up the way you did would affect you. The last thing I wanted to do was screw you up."

"You didn't. I'm good and happy to be closer to you."

"New York is a dangerous city. You need to be on guard at all times."

"Chicago wasn't any safer." I let out a light laugh.

We talked for a while, and then our time was up. The goodbye was always the hardest part.

"I'll see you next week." I smiled as we briefly hugged.

"Looking forward to it, sweetheart."

I walked out of the visiting room with an emptiness inside me. I hated seeing him locked up here. I thought that with each visit, it would get easier, but it never did.

"I'm ready to leave, Edmond," I softly spoke.

"Are you okay, Kate?"

"Not really."

We walked to the car, and I climbed inside, pulling my seat belt over my shoulder and buckling it.

"How about a macchiato and a blueberry muffin?" Edmond smiled.

"A blueberry muffin?"

"Didn't you know that blueberry muffins always chase the blues away?" He winked.

A smile crossed my lips, and we headed to Starbucks.

Chapter Twenty-Five

Kate

After returning to the townhouse, I went up to my room to soak in a bubble-filled warm tub before packing for our tomorrow morning trip. I wasn't sure what kind of mood Gabriel would be in when he got home since his anger and trust issues were getting worse, and I didn't feel like dealing with him. I lay my head back on the bath pillow and closed my eyes, taking in the sweet aroma of lavender. I was drifting into another world when I heard a loud knock on the bathroom door.

"Kate, are you in there?" Gabriel asked.

I opened my eyes and sighed. What was he doing home already?

"Yes."

I heard the turning of the knob, and the door opened. Gabriel stood there in his dark gray Armani suit, looking sexy as fuck.

"Do you mind?" I asked as I raised my brow.

"I don't." He smirked.

"Why are you home already? Shouldn't you be stressing out over something at the office?"

"I need to pack for Hawaii. I brought home dinner for us. I hope you're hungry."

"Depends on what you brought," I spoke with a slight attitude.

"Korean BBQ."

"I've never had it."

"There's a first time for everything. How much longer are you going to be? I don't want the food to get cold."

"I basically just got in before you knocked on the door."

"You can take one later. Get out and get dressed. Dinner is waiting," he spoke as he turned and walked away.

I took a sharp breath to try and stop the vulgar words from escaping my lips. Who the hell did he think he was telling me what to do? Unfortunately, instead of telling him to fuck off, I did as he asked. Not for him, but for me.

I went downstairs and found Gabriel sitting at the island and eating. Walking over to the fridge, I opened it and grabbed a bottle of water. I was unsure about the white food containers on the counter, even though they smelled amazing.

"So, what do we have here?" I asked.

"This container is pork belly. This one is duck, and this one is spicy beef short ribs."

I grabbed a plate and opted for the spicy beef short ribs. I wasn't a fan of duck, and there was no way I was eating pork belly. The thought sickened me.

"Taking the safe route, eh?" Gabriel smirked.

"Of course I am."

He seemed to be in a better mood than yesterday, which was good. The tension didn't seem as thick.

"What did you do today?" he asked.

Shit. Why did he have to ask?

"Not much," I lied. "Had a macchiato and a blueberry muffin with Edmond."

"You two seem to be getting along."

"I think he likes me now." I smiled.

"What else did you do? Did you get any packing done?"

"Not yet. I was going to start after my bath."

Damn. These spicy beef short ribs were amazing.

"This is why I can't trust you," he blurted out.

"Excuse me?"

"You lie every chance you get," he spoke in an irritated tone as he stuffed his face with pork belly.

"What are you talking about?"

"You went to visit your father at Rikers Island today. Didn't you?"

Dead silence filled the air. I was going to kill Edmond.

"Yes, I did." I gulped.

"Why didn't you say so?"

"How did you know? Did Edmond tell you? Because I specifically asked him not to."

He got up from his stool and took his plate to the sink.

"First of all, you are never to tell my employees to lie to me. EVER! Do you understand me? I have a tracker on the car. I monitor your activities all day long. I know exactly where you go."

I dropped my fork on my plate.

"Wow. Stalker much?"

"I wouldn't have to do it if you just told the truth all the time. Why didn't you want me to know you went to see him?"

"I don't know." I lowered my head.

"Damn it, Kate!" His fists slammed down on the counter. "Tell me why you wanted to hide it from me?"

"Whoa," Caleb spoke as he walked into the kitchen. "What's going on here?"

"Caleb, what are you doing here?" Gabriel asked in a calm tone.

"I just came to see you before you left for Hawaii tomorrow and to tell you that Sony Records offered us a solid contract!" He spoke with excitement.

"That's great. Congratulations." He smiled as he walked over and hugged his brother.

"Thanks."

"Congrats, Caleb. You guys deserve it."

He placed his hand on my shoulder. "Thanks, Kate. If this is a bad time—"

"No. Are you hungry?" Gabriel asked him.

"Nah. I just ate."

"Then come into the living room, and we'll have a celebratory drink. Kate, you may join us when you're finished eating."

"I'm not very hungry. I think I'll go up to my room and start packing." I got up from my stool and headed up the stairs without saying another word.

G abriel
"Mind telling me what all that was about?" Caleb spoke as we went into the living room.

Stepping behind the bar, I grabbed two glasses and a bottle of bourbon.

"She lied to me. She went to see her father today and tried to deny it."

"Why?"

"I don't know," I replied, handing him his drink.

"You normally aren't like this, bro. What's really going on?"

"Nothing. I want to know where she is and what she's doing at all times when she leaves this house."

"I never figured you to have stalker tendencies." He smirked.

"Now you sound like her." I rolled my eyes.

"You're in way too deep with her. Come on, Gabriel, this is me you're talking to."

"She just makes me so angry. More so now than before. I don't know." I shook my head.

"I'll tell you why." He took a sip of his drink. "It's because you've fallen for her and want her to be flawless. But that's not possible, bro. Everyone is flawed in one way or another. She's a con artist, but that's a front, a façade. You must look past that and deep into her heart and soul to find the person she's hiding."

I sat across from him with a puzzled look on my face. "What?"

"She's still playing all her roles, every person she ever invented. I believe she's scared shitless to show her true self."

"Why would she be afraid?" I asked.

"Stop and think about it for a minute. From the time she was a little girl, no one ever knew her by her real name. At least, that's what I'm assuming if her father was out conning people. When she met others, she had to become someone else, not Kate Harper. She never had the chance to be herself, bro, and I'm not sure she knows how. Or if she does, she's too afraid she won't be accepted."

I sighed as I brought my ankle to my knee and sipped my drink.

"Maybe you're right. I don't know."

"Something about her captivated you when you first saw her. And even though she was disguised as someone else that night of the gala, you knew it was her. And why?" he asked.

"Her smile."

"Exactly, bro. That smile belongs to Kate Harper and always has, no matter how many different people she has become. You already saw a real piece of her, which drew you to her in the first place. Give her a break and let the rest of the real Kate Harper emerge. She will. Trust me." He grinned.

"Are you sure your passion is with music?" I cocked my head.

"Yeah. I'm sure." He smirked. "You know I've always had this little gift of seeing through people. Anyway, thanks for the drink. I better get going. The band and I are heading to L.A. in a few days to record. I'm so stoked."

We both stood up, and I gave my brother a tight hug.

"I'm really happy for you, Caleb. Just don't forget about me when you're this huge off-the-charts rock star."

"Nah, bro. You're my fam and the most important person in my life. I love you."

"I love you too. Now get out of here." I patted his back.

Chapter Twenty-Six

K ate
As I was packing, there was a light knock on my door.

"Come in," I softly spoke.

"I see you're packing," Gabriel said as he entered the room.

"Yep."

I turned to the closet and grabbed a couple of sundresses I had purchased for the trip.

"By the way, how long will we be in Hawaii?" I asked.

"A few days. Why?"

"Just wondering how much I should pack."

"Listen, Kate. I want to apologize for earlier."

"Apology accepted," I spoke as I neatly folded the sundresses and put them in my suitcase. "Now, if you'll excuse me, I want to finish packing before coming to your room."

"About that. I think it would be best to take tonight off. I've had a long day, and so have you, and we both need our rest before our four a.m. flight."

"Four a.m.?" I cocked my head. "What time are we leaving the house?"

"Carl will be waiting outside for us at three."

"That doesn't give us enough time to get to the airport, check our bags, and go through security," I spoke.

"We aren't flying commercial. I've rented a private jet. Once we arrive in Hawaii around three o'clock, we have a couple of hours until we need to be down at the restaurant for a special grand opening dinner, so pack something formal."

"Why are you just telling me this now?" I glared at him. "I don't have anything formal here. All my dresses are back at my apartment."

He sighed. "I'll make a few calls and have some dresses waiting in the hotel suite when we arrive. What size are you?"

"Four."

"And shoe size?"

"Eight."

He got up from the bed.

"Get some rest, and I'll see you in a few hours," he spoke as he walked out the door, pulling it shut behind him.

My alarm woke me from a sound sleep at two thirty a.m. This was not normal to get up this early for a flight. I dragged my tired body out of bed, threw my hair up in a messy bun, and pulled on a pair of black leggings, a white Cami, and a long black cardigan. After slipping my feet into my black flats, I grabbed my suitcase and took it to the elevator. When I reached the foyer, Gabriel was already there, waiting.

"Good morning," he spoke.

"It's the middle of the night, and there's nothing good about waking up at this time," I snarled.

"You'll be fine." He handed me a silver travel mug. "I made you some coffee."

"Thanks."

The door opened, and both Carl and Edmond stepped inside.

"Edmond? You're going with us?"

"Yes." He smiled.

I glanced over at Gabriel.

"Did you really think I would let you on your own in Hawaii?" he asked with a raised brow. "I can't be with you at all times."

"That's fine." I walked over to Edmond and hooked my arm in his. "I like his company better anyway. Carl, grab my suitcase, please."

We climbed into the limo, and Gabriel sat across from me with an irritated look. I didn't care. Even though I told him I accepted his apology, I didn't. I was done trying to make him trust me. It wasn't worth it anymore. If he wanted to have an attitude with me, yell, and be mean, fine. I prayed to God to give me the strength to get through these next weeks and keep what little bit of sanity I had left.

~

G abriel
      She sat in the window seat, staring out into the clouds. Her eyes looked tired, and she still wouldn't say a word to me. I closed my laptop, got up from the couch, and sat beside her. With a slight turn of her head, she glared at me.

"Can I help you?" she asked with a cocky but tired attitude.

"I thought maybe we could talk."

"I'm too tired to carry on a conversation." She laid her head against the window.

I held out my hand to her.

"Come with me."

"Where?"

"There's a bedroom on this plane with a comfortable bed for you to sleep in."

"Where?" She sat up and looked around.

"In the back. Come on."

Her beautiful blue eyes stared into mine before she accepted my extended hand. I led her to the small but luxurious bedroom. She immediately kicked off her shoes and climbed on the bed, laying her head on the pillow.

"This is nice." She smiled as she closed her eyes.

I stretched out on the bed next to her and rested my back against the headboard, placing my hands behind my head.

"What are you doing?" she asked with one eye open.

"This is quite comfortable. I think I'll rest my eyes for a bit. Is that a problem?"

"Do you snore?" she asked.

"No. Do you?"

"No."

"Good. Go to sleep." My lips gave way to a small smile.

I kept my eyes closed for a few moments and then opened them as I stared at her beautiful, slightly parted lips and the rise and fall of her chest as she slept. Maybe Caleb was right. She was hiding herself, not only from the world but from me.

I was jolted out of a sound sleep. My eyes flew open to find Kate lying on her side, facing me and pinching my nose.

"What the hell, Kate?"

"You were snoring. You told me you didn't snore." She smirked.

"I don't," I spoke as I sat up.

"You do." The smirk never left her face.

I sighed as I rested my head back on the headboard.

"How long have we been asleep?" I asked.

"A couple of hours."

"I don't know about you, but I'm starving. How about I order us some lunch?"

I picked up the phone on the small round table next to the bed and told Darcy, the flight attendant, to bring in lunch.

"Also, bring in a bottle of wine and two glasses," I spoke.

"Coming right up, Mr. Quinn."

"We're eating in here?" she asked as she arched her brow.

"Yes. It's comfy. Plus, it's more private so that we can talk."

"Talk about what?" She sat up and crossed her legs.

"I know you didn't accept my apology last night. You're still mad."

"You're right." She looked down as she played with her hands. "Why is it so important to you to know about my visit to my father?"

"Maybe because I'm just trying to get to know you better. All I want is to know you, Kate. The real you. Not Hannah, who stole my watch, and not all the other people you were with other men."

Our moment was interrupted by a knock on the door.

"Come in." I sighed.

"Your lunch, sir," Darcy spoke as she wheeled in a silver cart with two plates, a bottle of wine, and two glasses.

"Thank you."

After pouring the wine, I handed Kate her glass along with her plate. We stretched out on the bed with our backs against the headboard, and I continued our conversation.

"I just want to know you."

A whisper of a laugh escaped her. "I've lived a lie my entire life, and once we moved to Chicago, I thought the lie had ended, and I could be Kate Harper for the first time. Then, my father went to prison, and the vicious cycle started all over again. I had the opportunity once to tell someone my real name. Carla was our neighbor next door to the house we rented. She was a sweet old woman in her eighties. You'd never know she was that old. She had the spunk of a girl in her twenties. When she introduced herself, my name was on the tip of my tongue. I was going to tell her, and then I'd be set free. Free from the pretending that I had done for so long and that someone in this big world would finally know who I was. But this little voice inside my head told me not to do it because anything could have and probably would have happened. I didn't completely trust myself or my situation to tell her that my name was Kate Harper. So, I introduced myself as Katerina Voight. Katie, for short. It was close enough to my first name, so it didn't feel so bad."

"I'm sorry you had to live like that, Kate."

She reached over to the table on her side and picked up her wine glass.

"It wasn't all bad."

"Why did you finally decide to tell me?" I asked.

"Because it felt right, and I want to gain your trust. Plus, you had kidnapped me and already knew all my aliases, so what was the point of not telling you?"

I let out a long sigh. "I didn't kidnap you. How many

times do I have to tell you that? You voluntarily came home with me."

A small smile crossed her lips.

"Then you locked me in a bedroom and secured the house so I couldn't leave. I would classify that as kidnapping. Not to mention the fact that you handcuffed me when we left the house, and you gave me a cell phone where your number was the only one I could dial."

"Okay." I held up my hand. When you say it like that—"

"I'm glad you finally realize what you've done." She smirked.

"It hasn't been that bad, has it?" I asked.

"Not so much. It's the most normal I've felt in my entire life."

"Really?" I cocked my head, and our eyes met. "Why?"

"Because I no longer had to pretend to be someone I wasn't." She looked down at her plate.

I reached over and softly stroked her cheek with my hand.

Chapter Twenty-Seven

K ate
I opened my soul to him at that very moment, and he didn't judge me. For the first time in my life, I felt normal. I brought my hand up to my cheek and placed it on his as I closed my eyes. The warmth of his touch radiated throughout my body and made me tremble. He took our plates and set them back on the cart. Turning to me, he cupped my chin in his hand and softly brushed his lips against mine. Our kiss soon turned passionate as I lay down, and he hovered over me. We made love. Slow, sensual, and in various positions before he exploded inside me. The gentle touch of his hands on my body sent chills down my spine. His touch felt possessive and made me feel safe and secure—a feeling I wanted to feel for the rest of my life.

We lay in bed for the first time together, his arms wrapped around me as my head laid on his chest.

"We should get back out there," he spoke. "I need to check my emails."

"Yeah. We should. How much longer is the flight?" I asked as I lifted my head.

"About three more hours." He softly kissed my lips.

I climbed off the bed and slipped back into my clothes. Gabriel did the same, and we both left the bedroom. He took his laptop to the table, and I sat back in my seat, staring at the clouds as the plane floated through them. I couldn't help but glance over at Gabriel now and again. And every time I did, the corners of my mouth curved up into a small smile. The anger I harbored towards him quickly dissipated when he explained why he was so angry with me. I got it. I really did, and the best part was that I trusted him. All the man wanted was honesty from the start, but I was too afraid to let the real me emerge.

When we finally landed, we took a limo that was waiting for us to the hotel, which consisted of ten floors, four hundred breathtaking guest rooms, six restaurants, a coffee café, a candy shop, a gift shop, a large gym, casual and formal clothing stores for men and women, and a luxurious spa.

"Wow," I spoke in amazement as we entered the marbled lobby.

"Welcome to Quinn Hotels, Kate." Gabriel smiled.

After being greeted by numerous staff and the hotel manager, Albert, we headed up to the penthouse suite on the tenth floor overlooking the ocean. I walked out to the terrace and took in Hawaii's beauty. The roaring of the ocean and the subtle sounds the waves made as they crashed to the shore gave me a sense of peace.

"Well, what do you think?" he asked as he walked up behind me.

"It's beautiful. The hotel, the room, everything."

"I designed this entire hotel myself. I had been working on it for a couple of years."

"Your father would be so proud." I smiled.

"Can I let you in on a little secret?" he asked.

"Of course."

"I'm going to build a digital hotel. The first one will be in Las Vegas, and we're projected to start building in about six months."

"Care to explain what a digital hotel consists of?" I smirked.

"Every guest room will have its own virtual butler who will control everything in the room from temperature control, lights, shades, showers, baths, and TVs. You name it, and the virtual butler will do it for you. He will even order room service for you. All you have to do is ask."

I let out a laugh. "Are you serious? So, what do I say if I want to take a shower?"

"For example, let's say your butler for your room is named Gregory. You would say, 'Gregory, I want to take a shower.' The shower will turn on automatically before you even walk into the bathroom."

"Shut up." I lightly smacked him.

"I'm serious. Each room will have a huge computer screen attached to the wall. You don't even have to sit down and type anything out if you want to surf the web or check your emails. The butler will do it for you. For example, you'd say, 'Gregory, I need to check my email,' and voila, your emails will appear on the screen. You can also check out. 'Gregory, I'm checking out at nine a.m.,' and you will automatically be checked out at that time."

"Does Gregory talk back?" I asked.

"Of course. When you enter the room, he'll greet you. When you leave the room, he'll tell you goodbye. You can carry on a conversation with him to an extent. He'll ask you how your day was, if you slept well, and tell you good morning."

"That's kind of creepy." I scrunched up my nose. "I'm surprised you aren't having a sexy woman's voice."

"Ah." He smiled. "If a man travels alone, his butler/maid will be female. But if it's a couple, it will be male."

I rolled my eyes at him. "Of course. It sounds amazing."

"It will be. My father had always dreamed of it. Before he died, he told me to make sure I built it. It was a project he had been working on for ten years. Vegas will be the first place to launch it."

"I'm going to assume it will also be a casino?"

"Of course, it will be. One of the best Vegas has to offer." He smiled. "Listen," he took hold of my hands, "only five people know about this, including you. We are the only company with that kind of technology for this right now, and word can't get out. Understand?"

"Sure. I would never tell a soul. You, of all people, know how good I am at keeping secrets."

"I know." He kissed my forehead. "We should get ready for dinner. Your dresses should be in the bedroom. Go pick one out while I get in the shower."

When I walked into the beautifully decorated bedroom, there was a silver rack in the corner with approximately ten different dresses hanging upon it. Shoes were laid out in front of the rack, coordinating with each dress. I thumbed through the rack and pulled out a champagne-colored gown with ornate beading and a layered A-line bottom. It was perfect. I took my makeup into the bathroom of the other bedroom, took a shower, and got ready. After curling my hair, I pinned it up but left a few wispy curls hanging. After slipping into my dress and putting on the matching shoes with a heel, I walked out into the suite's living area and saw Gabriel standing on the terrace with a drink in his hand. His eyes raked over me from head to toe.

"You look stunning." He smiled as he walked towards me.

"And so do you. I smiled as I straightened his bow tie.

"Shall we?" He held out his arm.

"We shall, Mr. Quinn."

We took the elevator down to Incognito, one of the formal restaurants in the hotel. The place was filled with influential businessmen and women. We mixed and mingled for a while as he introduced me as Kate. I was grateful he didn't tell my last name. I wasn't ready for the world to know me yet. I was still getting used to Gabriel knowing who I was.

While he talked business with some friends, I sat at the bar.

"What can I get you?" the polite bartender asked.

"Tequila with a splash of lime, please."

"Coming right up." He smiled.

As I was sipping on my drink, I noticed a man take the seat next to me.

"I'll have what the pretty lady is having," he spoke with a French accent to the bartender. "May I buy you another?" A grin crossed his lips.

I studied him. Mid-forties, stylish blonde hair, which he dyed, and short on the sides with a shag on top. Green eyes that had a shady look about them. Wealthy and slick. French. A player. A definite player.

"Sure. Why not." I smiled.

"My name is Marcel Mathieu." He extended his hand.

"Kate." I placed mine in his and gave it a light shake.

"Why is a beautiful woman like yourself sitting alone at the bar? I would never let you out of my sight if you were my wife."

He was trying to find out if I was single and making himself sound like a stalker.

"I'm not married." I smiled.

"Well then, if I were your boyfriend, I would never let you out of my sight." He gave his head a light nod.

"No boyfriend either." I took a sip of my drink.

"I find that hard to believe." He smirked.

"Well, believe it." I arched my brow.

"Whom are you here with? Don't tell me you're at this beautiful hotel alone."

"I'm here with Gabriel Quinn."

"I see. Well, it was nice to meet you, Kate." He got up from his stool.

"Nice to meet you too, Marcel. Thanks for the drink." I held up my glass.

Was it something I said? Gabriel walked over and placed his hand on my back.

"What was that all about?" he asked.

"Marcel?" I turned my head and looked at him.

"Yes."

"He was hitting on me, bought me a drink, and then he bolted when he found out I was here with you. What's going on there?"

Gabriel took the seat Marcel had sat in and asked the bartender for a bourbon.

"His father and mine were rivals. Had been for years. It started with our grandfathers."

"What happened?" I asked.

"When my grandfather first had the idea to open a hotel, he was short of funds. He and Marcel's grandfather had been friends for years at that time. He offered to loan my grandfather the additional money he needed to open the hotel in exchange for being his business partner. My grandfather agreed, and soon after, QM Quarters was opened. At first, it didn't do so well and was almost forced into bankruptcy after the first year."

"Why?" I frowned.

"Because Marcel's grandfather's vision changed, and he wanted more too fast. He wanted to be on top and number one. He became greedy. So, to get him out of the company, my grandfather blackmailed him."

"With what?"

"I don't know. My father never would tell me, but it had to be something serious for Marcel's grandfather to accept the buyout. That was the end of their partnership and friendship. His grandfather packed his family up, moved back to France, and opened his own hotel, which does very well. After he passed away, Marcel's father decided it was time to move out of France and here to New York, where he opened up his first hotel in the U.S."

"Which hotel chain does he own?"

"Regal Hotels."

"Big competition for you?" I smiled as I sipped my drink.

"Not really. They do a good business, but nothing like my hotels do. Enough talk about Marcel. Let's go sit down for dinner." He held out his arm.

Chapter Twenty-Eight

Gabriel

I watched her from across the room as she stood and spoke with some of the guests. Everyone seemed to like her. She radiated beauty and confidence, and she turned me on. My feelings for her came full force today after she opened up to me. I considered it a breakthrough, and it made me happy that she trusted me enough to tell me about her life. It was getting late, and the last of the guests left the restaurant.

"Are you ready to head up to the room?" I asked her as she sat at the bar.

She stumbled as she attempted to get up.

"Whoa." I smiled as I grabbed her arm. "I think you had one too many tequilas."

"Nah." She waved her hand in front of her face. "I'm fine."

She held on to my arm, and as we began to take a few steps, she stopped.

"The room is spinning, and I'm not feeling so well," she softly spoke.

I swooped her up and carried her to the elevator.

"Lay your head on my shoulder and close your eyes," I spoke. "And please, whatever you do, do not get sick on me."

"I'll try not to." She closed her eyes.

Once we reached the suite, I opened the door and began to carry her to the guest bedroom but stopped midway, turned around, and carried her to the master suite. Laying her on the bed, I removed her shoes, rolled her over, and unzipped her dress. Grabbing the robe from the closet, I laid it on the bed while taking off her dress.

"Gabriel?" she spoke as she looked at me.

"Yes?"

"I think I'm going to be sick."

"Shit."

I grabbed hold of her arm, quickly led her to the bathroom, and rubbed her shoulders as she vomited all the alcohol she drank. Once she was done, I ran a washcloth under cool water and placed it on her forehead.

"Do you normally get sick like this when you drink?"

"No. It must have been those fireball shots I was doing."

"Fireball shots? With whom?" I asked.

"I think her name was Lydia. Or was it Lucy? Or maybe it was Lulu. Hell, I don't remember."

I smiled as I helped her from the floor and into bed. Climbing in next to her, I told her good night and turned off the light. As I drifted off to sleep, I heard Kate's voice.

"I've been lying to my father for years," she whispered.

I opened my eyes and turned my head to look at her.

"What?"

"He doesn't know what I've been doing since he went to prison."

I sat up, reached over, and turned on the lamp.

"Kate, I don't understand."

She rolled over to face me and tucked her hands under her pillow.

"He thinks I was working at a high-end restaurant as a waitress and attending school in Chicago. When I went to visit him the other day, I told him that I had just moved here because the owner I worked for opened a restaurant in New York, and I asked him if I could transfer so I could be closer to him. If he knew what I had done, he'd be so disappointed. The last thing he said to me before they sent him to prison was, 'Don't make the same mistakes I did. Go out into the world and make something of yourself. Make your old man proud.'"

I lay down on my pillow, facing her, and stroked her cheek.

"You were doing what you thought you had to do to get him out of prison. Maybe it's time you told him the truth."

"I don't think I can. I couldn't bear to see the disappointment in his eyes."

"He loves you, Kate. You're his entire world. Sure, he'll be upset and disappointed for a while, but his love for you will overtake that."

"Your father's love for Caleb didn't overtake it."

"My father was a different man and incapable of truly loving anyone. He let his success and greed consume him. All he really cared about was his reputation."

She moved closer and snuggled under my arm, forcing me to lie on my back so her head could rest against my chest. I slowly closed my eyes as I kissed the top of her head.

"The one thing I always wanted growing up was a dog. A white Maltese so I could put cute little bows on her head. But with the way we moved around so much, my dad said it wasn't a good idea. I always thought that having a dog of my own would make me feel less lonely. I need to sleep now," she whispered.

"Get some rest. We can talk about this more in the morning."

Her wall was crumbling before me, and I'd be there for her when the last piece fell. She was growing more important to me with each truth than I thought she would. Holding her against me felt right, more than anything in my life. I'd held many women beside me in bed, but holding her gave me a new feeling. One I couldn't describe. I closed my eyes and drifted off into a deep sleep.

Today was the official grand opening of the hotel, and every room in the place was booked. Now that this was finished, my attention and focus would go heavily into building the new hotel in Vegas, which was the most important to me. I had people to speak with and a couple of meetings to hold, so I told Kate to go do whatever she wanted, and I'd catch up with her later. She chose to go down to the beach for the day. She said that if she couldn't see parts of Hawaii with me, she'd be happy to sit in the sand under the warm sun and wait for me. I believed her and could honestly say I was fully starting to trust her.

"We need to get dressed and go down for breakfast. Are you feeling okay?"

"I am. I'm going to take a quick shower first if we have time," she spoke.

"Good idea. Let's take one together to save time." I smiled.

"I'd like that." She bit into her bottom lip.

She climbed out of bed, and with her back to me, she slid her robe off her body, letting it fall to the floor. Her curves and perfectly round ass made my cock stand in an instant. She walked into the bathroom, climbed into the shower, and I followed.

Our lips tenderly met as we stood under the stream of warm water. My hands groped her breasts as hers wrapped around my hard cock, stroking it up and down, causing me to become more excited than I already was. Getting down on my knees, my tongue slid down her torso while my hands stayed firmly planted on her breasts, down her clit, and to her aroused, wet opening. I circled around her as moans escaped her lips. Moans of pleasure and fulfillment. Dipping a finger inside, I explored her until I knew she was ready to take my cock inside her. I couldn't wait anymore, and the animal inside me was about to emerge. Standing up, I placed her against the shower wall, grabbing her ass tightly and lifting her up onto my cock. Her arms and legs wrapped around me, and our lips passionately met. The water beat down on us as I thrust inside her. She took me all in, every inch, with ease. The warmth was overwhelming and intoxicating. Our moans were in sync as we enjoyed the pleasure we gave each other. I thrust in and out of her rapidly, holding her tight and against my wet body. She came, and I smiled as our lips were connected. One last thrust and I buried myself inside, straining to pour every drop of come I had in her. I was changing, she was changing, and the feeling that resided inside me couldn't have been more right.

"Thank you," she whispered as our eyes locked on each other.

"You're welcome." I smiled.

"I don't mean about what just happened. I mean for being there for me and listening."

"Again, you're welcome. I'm here for you any time you need me, Kate. Never forget that."

"I won't." Her lips pressed against mine.

"We better wash up and get out of here," I spoke.

I set her down, and she grabbed the shampoo bottle, poured some into her hands, and placed them on my head. We laughed and joked around as we washed each other. I didn't want the shower to end, but we needed to head downstairs by the time all was said and done.

Chapter Twenty-Nine

Kate

After breakfast, Gabriel had business stuff to do, so Edmond and I headed down to the beach.

"Can I let you in on a little secret?" I asked him.

"Sure." He smiled.

"I love him, Edmond. For the first time in my life, I'm in love."

He reached over and took hold of my hand, which shocked the shit out of me.

"I know you do, and I'm pretty sure Mr. Quinn has the same feelings for you."

"You think?" I looked over at him.

"Yes, I do."

"I don't know. A man like him could never love someone like me. I've done horrible things."

"Listen, Kate. Don't beat yourself up about the things you've done. Put it all in the past and live in the present. Love doesn't come around very often. When it does, you must hold on to it as tightly as possible. Because if you don't, you'll live a life full of regrets."

"Is that what you're doing?" I asked. "Were you in love once?"

He let go of my hand and sighed.

"I was stupid and let love walk right out of my life. Once I realized what I had done, I told her I was wrong and couldn't live without her. I stopped at the flower shop and bought her a dozen red roses. I made a dinner reservation at her favorite restaurant, and I was going to ask for her hand in marriage. She was running some errands that day and agreed to meet with me when she was finished. She said she'd call when she got home. I waited for hours, and I still hadn't heard from her. I tried calling her phone, but it kept going straight to voicemail. Then my phone rang, and her sister told me that Vivian had been in a car accident and was taken to the hospital. By the time I got there, she had already passed away."

"Oh my god, Edmond. I'm so sorry." I placed my hand on his.

"If you love him, hold on to him. Don't let self-doubt and fear keep you from happiness. Believe me, Kate. It's the worst feeling in the world when you let the one you love go and never get the chance to tell them you were wrong."

He got up from the sand. "I'm going to get a drink. Want one?"

"That would be great. Just water for me, though."

As I sat there with my eyes closed, reflecting on what Edmond had told me, I heard a man's voice with a French accent beside me.

"Well, hello again."

Looking at him through my sunglasses, I spoke, "Hello."

"How is your day going so far?" he asked.

"Fine. And yours?"

"Very good now that I see this beautiful woman alone on the beach."

"I'm not alone. My friend Edmond is with me. He just went to get me some water."

"No Gabriel today?"

"He's busy doing work stuff. By the way, I didn't get a chance to ask you last night since you hastily ran away. What are you doing here?"

"Gabriel is a friend of mine, and I wanted to congratulate him on opening his beautiful hotel."

This guy was full of shit. I could smell it a mile away.

"Are you and Gabriel an item? Because last night, you said you didn't have a boyfriend."

"I don't, and no, we aren't an item. Just good friends."

"That pleases me to hear that. How about joining me for dinner this evening?" he spoke.

"As much as I would enjoy that, Marcel, I'm afraid I can't. I have dinner plans with Gabriel. What kind of friend would I be to cancel to have dinner with you?"

"Understood. A woman who values her friendships. I like that." He smirked. "I'm flying back to New York tomorrow. Perhaps we can do something before I leave."

"I'm not sure that's going to be possible. Have a safe flight home." I smiled.

"A woman who plays hard to get is a turn-on. Make no mistake, Kate, we will have dinner together one day. I always go after what I want." He stood up and gave me a wink. Before he walked away, he turned and looked at me. "By the way, I never got your last name."

"Young. Kate Young." I smiled.

"I will find you, Kate Young," he spoke as he walked away.

I sat there, shaking my head in disbelief. What a tool.

"Again?" Gabriel asked as he stood over me, handing me a bottle of water.

"What are you doing here? I thought you had business stuff to do."

"I did, and then I said screw it. I think we should spend the day together."

"Where's Edmond?"

"I ran into him as he was getting your water and told him to explore Hawaii. On me, of course."

He held out his hand and helped me up from the sand.

"What did Marcel want this time?"

"He wanted me to join him for dinner tonight. I told him no and that I had plans with you. That guy is a real asshole."

"I know he is, and I don't want you talking to him. He's trouble."

"No worries. He's leaving tomorrow to go back to New York."

"Good. The only reason he's here is to spy so he can steal ideas. The man and his father are as crooked as they come. Guess what?"

"What?" I asked.

"I'm taking you on a yacht for the day."

"I get seasick." I smirked.

"I don't really care." He pulled me into him and kissed my lips.

Gabriel and I spent the next few days exploring Hawaii and enjoying each other's company. Each day, we grew closer, and my feelings for him strengthened. I had never felt this way before, and honestly, it scared me a little because it was all too perfect. I wanted to tell him I loved him, but I wanted to wait for him to say it first. Even though I was pretty sure he did, a part of me was scared to death of rejection. This was the kind of life I had always dreamed of. Being me, Kate Harper, and no one else. I decided that I would tell my father the truth when we went home to New York. He needed to know, and I needed to tell him for my own sake. My days of living as a con were over. I was going to focus on getting a real job and live my life for me.

It was our last night in Hawaii, and Gabriel and I walked hand in hand on the beach along the shore. We stopped momentarily and took in the beauty of the sun that had begun to set over the ocean.

"I've decided that when we get back, I'm going to tell my father the truth," I spoke.

"Really?"

"Really." I smiled. "It's time I take control of my life. I've been living in my father's shadow my entire life, doing everything he told me to do, and still doing it after he went to prison."

"I don't understand. Your father didn't want you to do what you did. You made that choice."

"I did it for him so he wouldn't have to spend twenty years in prison. Being alone in a world where not one single person except him knew who I truly was, was frightening. It was easier to be all those different people, so I didn't have to face the reality of being myself all alone in the world."

He wrapped his arms around me and pulled me into him.

"You aren't alone, Kate. You have me." He kissed the top of my head. "And Edmond. Let's not forget about him."

A smile crossed my lips as I broke our embrace and looked up at him. Hues of rich orange, yellow, and red shadowed him. To me, he was my savior.

"Thank you, Gabriel. That means so much to me."

He swept his thumb across my lips before his mouth met mine amongst the ocean's shores and underneath the sunset.

Chapter Thirty

G abriel
Hawaii was perfect, and Kate and I were growing closer every day. She was desperate to change her life, and I trusted her. I told her that I would help her in every way I could, and if she wanted a job at my offices, she had one. She wasn't sure what she wanted to do with her life. She was still learning how to be herself, and I couldn't be prouder. I loved her. I was in love with her, and she took up every bit of space I had in my heart.

Our thirty days were almost up, and even though the original plan was to let her go, I couldn't. I wanted her to stay in my life and make her mine and mine only. The words "I love you" were on the tip of my tongue every day, but I had to hold back because I didn't want to scare her. I had a plan. On day thirty, I would spend the day with her, buy her beautiful flowers, take her somewhere special, and profess my love. It had to be perfect. I wouldn't have it any other way. This love was real for me this time. I had it all. A thriving business and career I loved, a beautiful home, family, friends, and a woman whom I adored and loved with every fiber of my soul. Sex with her was out of this world. She even let me use the handcuffs on her. In fact, she was the one who suggested it. She pleased me in every way possible. I wanted to take care of her, but I knew she needed to figure out what she wanted first for her to let me. I knew she loved me. Even though she hadn't said it, I could feel it.

I held her in my arms, her body wrapped tightly around mine as we lay in bed. Today was the day she was going to tell her father the truth. I asked her if she wanted me to go with her, and she said she wanted to go alone. I kissed the top of her head, thankful that she was with me.

"Morning." She smiled as she opened her eyes.

"I didn't mean to wake you," I spoke.

"You didn't." Her finger ran across my chest.

"I have to get ready for work. Are you sure you don't want me to go with you to see your father?"

"I'm sure. This is something I need to do on my own. But the next time I visit him, I would love for you to go." She lifted her head and brushed her lips against mine.

"I would like that."

I kissed her one last time, got up, hopped into the shower, and got ready for work. Before leaving for the office, we enjoyed a nice breakfast together, like we did every morning.

"Have a good day." She smiled as she kissed me goodbye.

"You too, sweetheart. Good luck with your dad."

I spent a better part of the day in back-to-back meetings, and when I returned to my office, Thaddeus walked in, and instantly, I knew something was wrong.

"You better sit down, Gabriel," he spoke.

"What's going on?" I asked as I narrowed my eyes.

178

He threw an article on my desk. I picked it up, and as I read it, my heart began to pound rapidly.

"What the fuck is this?" I asked through gritted teeth as my grip on the paper tightened.

"I—I don't know."

I stood up from my chair and slammed my fists down on the desk. Rage consumed me.

"Where did you get this?"

"It was sent by messenger when you were in your meetings," he replied. "How is this possible? Did you—"

I ran my hands through my hair as I paced around my office.

"Of course not!" I shouted. "FUCK! Get everyone in my office now!"

I took off my suitcoat, threw it on the chair, and continued to pace around the office in disbelief. Thaddeus walked back in with my team and sat at the table. I grilled them one by one. I yelled, screamed, and showed them a side of me they'd never seen before. I trusted them and their answers. Then, something hit me. It had to be her. My staff would never betray me, but I wouldn't put it past someone else. I didn't want to believe it. I couldn't believe it. But it had started to make sense. I grabbed my suitcoat and flew out of the office.

"Lu, I'm going home. I'll see you tomorrow," I spoke as I rushed past her.

Before walking through the front door, I took three deep breaths to calm down. As I stepped inside, I called her name.

"What are you doing home?" Kate asked as she walked down the stairs.

"I have a question for you and want an honest answer," I spoke harshly.

"Gabriel, what's wrong?" she asked as she approached me.

"Did you tell Marcel about my plans for the digital hotel?"

Her face fell instantly, and a look of fear swept over her.

"Of course not. Why would you—"

I reached into my pocket and pulled out the article.

"Because of this!"

She took it from me and began to read it.

"And you think I was the one who told him?"

"I certainly know my team would never do it." I placed my hands in my pocket. "You talked to him, Kate. Don't you find it odd that I would receive this article a week after we returned from Hawaii? After you talked to him!" I pointed at her.

"Gabriel," she spoke, panicked as she walked towards me.

I backed away and put my hands up. "Don't, Kate. Just admit you told him."

"I didn't tell him anything. I promised you I wouldn't say a word to anyone."

"Then how the fuck did he find out?!" I shouted.

"Stop yelling at me!" she shouted back. "I don't know. But it wasn't from me!"

"Did he make you some sweet offer you couldn't refuse? What a fucking fool I was for trusting someone like you!"

Tears streamed down her face.

"That was my father's dream! We were all set to announce it in a couple of months, and now, Marcel's company got to it first. And what a coincidence, theirs happens to be in Las Vegas."

"Gabriel, please. I didn't tell him." She begged.

Part of me wanted to believe her, but I quickly shut that

down because of her past. I turned my back, for I couldn't face her anymore.

"Get out," I firmly spoke.

"What?"

"Pack your stuff and get out of my house. I'm done with you."

"Gabriel, no," she cried as she grabbed my arm.

I jerked away so hard she fell to the ground.

"Don't come near me. You played me for a fool for the last time. I'm going out, and when I get back, you better be gone. Go back to your apartment and back to your con artist life. I better never see you again."

Chapter Thirty-One

Kate

He walked out, and it felt like the wind had been knocked out of me. The air I tried to breathe was so constricted that I felt like I was suffocating. I sat on the floor, my arms around my legs, rocking back and forth as tears fell from my eyes. This wasn't happening. The pain I felt inside was unbearable, and I began to hyperventilate. I didn't know what to do. It felt like my heart had been torn in half. After a while, as I tried to calm down, I picked myself up from the floor and stumbled up the stairs, one by one, in a daze, until I reached the bedroom and packed all my things. Once I was finished, I took the phone he gave me out of my purse and set it down on his bed. I had thought about writing him a letter of some sort, telling him once again that I didn't say a word to Marcel or anyone about his plans. But then I thought it wouldn't have mattered anyway. He never trusted me like he said he did. Way back in the dark corners of his mind, there was always doubt. Taking the elevator down to the foyer, I dragged my suitcase behind me in one hand, my guitar in the other, and out the front door.

When I reached my apartment, I unlocked the door and stepped inside. Turning on the lights, I stood in the small foyer and looked around the place I didn't want to be in. I wanted to be back at Gabriel's townhouse, sitting on the couch, snuggled up against him while we watched TV. I didn't know how to stop the overwhelming sadness, so I drowned my sorrows with a bottle of wine.

～

Gabriel

I had Carl park the limo around the corner, but just far enough away so I could watch her as she left. The feeling of betrayal I felt killed me inside. She said she didn't do it, and as much as I wanted to believe her, I couldn't. Once she left, I walked up the steps and through the front door. I went up to my bedroom and found her phone lying on the bed. I picked it up, and in a rage, I threw it against the wall. Pulling my phone from my pocket, I called my brother Caleb, who was in California recording his album.

"Hey, bro. Can I call you back in a few? We're just wrapping up."

"Sure. Do me a favor and Facetime me. I need to talk to you."

"Are you okay?" he asked.

"No, I'm not." I ran my hand down my face.

"Did something happen? Is Mom okay?"

"She's fine. It's about Kate."

"Shit. Okay. Give me about ten minutes."

I headed downstairs, poured myself a bourbon, downed

it, and took the bottle with me to my office. Opening my laptop, I waited for Caleb's call. A few moments later, my phone rang, and I explained what happened.

"Gabriel, are you one hundred percent sure Kate was the one who leaked it?"

"It's a gut feeling, Caleb. No one on my design team would betray me like that. There's too much at stake for them."

"Then what would Kate's reasoning be?"

"All I know is they talked quite a bit in Hawaii, and it was after I told her about my plans."

"So what if they talked? Marcel will talk to anything with long legs just to get a good fuck out of them. It doesn't mean she told him anything."

"And it doesn't mean she didn't."

"I thought you were over your trust issues with her," he spoke.

"I guess not. She played me. She gained my trust, only to stab me in the back."

"Bro, be careful with your words. You don't know that, and you don't have proof."

"Her past is all the proof I need. I'm sorry I ever got involved with her. God, I'm so fucking stupid."

"Calm the fuck down, Gabriel. You're not stupid. You just told me the other day about how in love with her you were and how she makes your life so much better. Now, the second something goes wrong, you automatically conclude she did it. Unless you have proof, it's not valid."

"Then I'll get proof." I pointed at the computer screen.

"How?"

"I don't know yet, but I will. Maybe she didn't do it on purpose, or it was just a mention, but I told her not to say a word to anyone."

He let out a long sigh.

"I'm sorry this happened. I really am. But I can't agree with you on this unless you know. And also, why are you letting Dad's dream destroy your life?"

"I'm not." I leaned back in my chair.

"You are. You're still catering to him, even after he's dead. The man was an emotional abuser, and you know it. And even though he's buried deep in the ground, he's still controlling you."

"You're being ridiculous, Caleb."

"No, Gabriel." He pointed at me. "You are. It's as if there aren't enough billion-dollar Quinn Hotels and Resorts in the world already. Why is this one so fucking important to you? I'll tell you why. It's because you're still trying to make him proud, just like you've done your entire life, following him around like a lost puppy. I was the only one in the family with enough guts to stand up to him and tell him exactly how I felt. Look at me, Gabriel. I'm happy, and you're miserable."

"Now you're just being a dick."

"Listen, bro, I'm sorry that you're going through this. You know I always have your back, but I'm not so sure in this case. I have to go. Tomorrow is our last day of recording, and then we're heading back to New York. I'll call you when I get in."

"Have a safe flight," I spoke as I hit the end button.

Chapter Thirty-Two

Kate

As hard as I tried to open my swollen eyes, I couldn't. They were sealed shut from all the crying I did last night, plus the pounding of my head from the bottle of wine I drank. I lay there, still distraught and in disbelief that my entire world crumbled before me in a split second. Tears started to creep out from the corner of my closed eyes. I didn't think I had any tears left, but every time I thought about him, they started back up again. I felt paralyzed and couldn't bring myself out of bed.

Three days later, after hibernating in my bed, only getting up to use the bathroom and get something to drink, I finally managed to take a bath. As I sunk into the rose-scented bubbles, I recalled my last visit with my father.

"Daddy, there's something I need to tell you," I spoke as I looked down from the embarrassment of lying to him the past few years.

"What is it, baby girl?" he asked with concern.

I told him everything, and his eyes filled with tears.

"My god, Kate. I have no words for what you just told

186

me. I'm so sorry." He slowly shook his head as the tears steadily ran down his face.

We talked for as long as we could until our time was up. Before I left, he hugged me tight.

"Go live a normal life, baby. That's all I want for you. I'm fine in here," he whispered in my ear.

I told him all about Gabriel and how happy I was. Now I'd have to go and tell my father what happened. I should have expected it. Life was too good, and I didn't deserve to be happy after everything I had done. This was karma paying me back for all those men I conned. I climbed out of the bathtub and slipped into my robe. I wasn't hungry, but I knew I had to eat something since I hadn't eaten in three days. I opened my freezer, which was about the only thing with some food, and pulled out a frozen pizza. As I preheated the oven, the buzzer to my apartment rang. Who the hell would be visiting me? The thought that it was Gabriel made me panic.

"Can I help you?" I asked over the intercom.

"Kate, it's me, Caleb. Can I come up?"

"Caleb? Sure. I'll buzz you in."

Confused, I opened the door and watched him step off the elevator.

"Hey." He gave me a sympathetic smile. "How are you?"

"Not good. Come on in. I'm making a frozen pizza. Would you care to join me?"

"Umm. No thanks. When was the last time you ate?"

"I don't know. Three days ago," I replied.

He pulled his phone from his pocket.

"Put that away. I'm going to order us a real pizza." He smiled.

"Caleb, I—"

"No arguments. I'm ordering it, and you're going to eat it."

He placed the pizza order and then followed me to the couch.

"How did you know where I live?" I asked.

"I had Carl drive me over."

"And Gabriel was okay with that?"

"My brother doesn't know and doesn't need to."

"He wouldn't be very happy knowing you're here."

"I don't care. It's none of his business whom I choose to visit."

I gave him a small smile as I played with the tie to my robe.

"Kate, I want you to look me straight in the eye and tell me the truth," he spoke with seriousness.

"I swear to you that I didn't tell Marcel or anyone about Gabriel's plans."

He reached over and placed his hand on mine.

"I believe you."

"Why? Why would you?"

"Because I know you wouldn't do anything to hurt Gabriel. You love him, and that right there says enough."

The buzzer rang and interrupted our conversation.

"That must be the pizza guy. I'll be right back," Caleb spoke as he got up from the couch and left the apartment.

I took a couple of plates from the cabinet and set them on the table. Caleb believed me, and that meant a lot. I'd just wished Gabriel would've. After a few moments, Caleb returned to my apartment with the pizza. Taking it over to the table, he set it down and opened the lid.

"Smells delicious," I spoke.

"It sure does. I'm starving." He smiled.

"Can I ask you something?" I spoke as I grabbed a slice of pizza and put it on my plate.

"You can ask me anything," he replied.

I asked the question I wasn't sure I wanted to know the answer to.

"How is Gabriel?"

"Upset. A mess. Pissed off at the world."

"I'm sorry." I looked down.

"Don't be, Kate. It's not your fault. Even though my brother thinks it is, it's not. He had no right to accuse you without proof. That should have been good enough for him if you said you didn't do it."

"He never has and never will trust me."

"Then that's his problem, isn't it? He always followed what our father said and did. He probably would have if he had told Gabriel to jump off a building. He was always so worried about disappointing him. Me, on the other hand," he smiled, "I didn't care. This is my life, and I would do what made me the happiest."

"You don't think Gabriel's happy running the company?" I asked as I took a bite of my pizza.

"He is in his own way. He was born to run a business. He's extremely smart and very skillful. The digital hotel isn't that big of a deal. He only wants to do it to please our father, even though he's buried six feet into the ground. You want to know what I think?"

"What?"

"I think someone in his company spilled the beans to Marcel."

"But why would anyone do that?" I asked.

"I don't know. Gabriel has known those people for years, and he trusts them. The thought that anyone would betray him is ludicrous to him. Unfortunately, you got caught in the crossfire. Have you ever met Thaddeus?"

"Not formally. He said hello to me once at Gabriel's office. But I've heard him mention his name a few times."

"I never trusted that guy. Something was always off about him. But Gabriel considers him a friend and a valuable asset to the company. He's his right-hand man even though I know if the opportunity arose, he'd stab my brother in the back."

Thoughts were flying through my head like a swarm of birds flying south for the winter.

"Tell me more about Thaddeus."

"Why?" he asked with a narrowed eye.

A moment of silence filled the air.

"Kate, no."

"What?" I took another slice of pizza from the box.

"I know what you're thinking, and it won't work."

"It will. Maybe he was the one who told Marcel."

"Just leave it alone. Gabriel fucked up with you in a big way. He made his bed. Now let him lie in it."

"The only important thing to me is proving that I didn't do anything."

"And how are you going to do that?"

"I don't know yet. But I do know that someone in that office betrayed Gabriel, and if they did it once, they'd do it again."

"Why do you care so much?" Caleb asked.

"Because I'm not being blamed for something I didn't do. I've done a lot of shit in my life and am the first to admit it. But this. Having my whole life ripped apart for something I didn't do is unacceptable."

"Okay. So let's say you prove it was someone Gabriel works with. Then what? Are you hoping to get him back?"

"No. What Gabriel and I had is over with for good. He's proven that he could never trust me. His words were horrible, and I don't think I could ever forgive him for that. I need a fresh start. A place where nobody knows Kate Harper. A place where I can start a new life."

"As a con?" His brow arched.

A small smile crossed my lips.

"No. Those days are over."

"Any idea what you want to do with your life?" he asked.

"Not really. But I know I need to get a job wherever I move."

"Kate, don't leave New York because of Gabriel. There are so many opportunities here for you."

"Like what?"

"Since you like to paint, get a job at an art gallery."

"I can paint, but I don't know much about art." I smiled. "Plus, being in the same city as him will be too hard. It's just best that I move somewhere else and make a fresh start for myself."

"What about your dad?"

"He'll want me to do what's best for me, and I'll still visit him."

Caleb reached over and took hold of my hand.

"Do what makes you happy, but don't be a stranger to me. Okay?"

"Okay." I smiled.

"I better get going." He got up from his seat.

"Thank you for the pizza, Caleb, and for checking on me."

"No problem, Kate. You have a lot of talents. Choose one and follow your heart." He kissed my cheek as I walked him to the door.

As soon as he left, I put my plan into motion. Grabbing my laptop, I did some googling and found out who Thaddeus Wilson was. If he weren't the person who told Marcel about the hotel, I would have to go after Marcel myself.

Chapter Thirty-Three

Gabriel
I thought about her day and night. I didn't want to, but it seemed everything I saw reminded me of her. I tried so hard to get her out of my head, which drove me crazy. A part of me missed her. The fun we had, the laughs we shared, and the side of her she finally let out. But she would always have that other side. The side that manipulated people to get what she wanted. The side that lied over and over again.

"Gabriel," Marcel spoke as he sat across from me at Daniel, where I invited him for dinner.

"Marcel."

"I was pleasantly surprised to have received a phone call from you, let alone have you invite me to dinner."

"I never did thank you for coming to the grand opening of my hotel."

"You're welcome." He grinned. "It was my pleasure. I was already in Hawaii, so I thought I'd stop by and show some support."

"Really?" I arched my brow. "Our families have hated each other for years."

He shrugged. "Times have changed. We now run our families' companies. Maybe it's time to put an end to what our grandfathers started. This war," he waved his hand, "is ridiculous. We both run very successful companies. There's no need for any more hostility, Gabriel. I think the two of us can start new traditions for our future families."

I wanted to reach across the table and grab him by his throat. No way in hell would ever happen.

"Maybe you're right," I lied.

"Now, tell me the real reason you wanted to meet for dinner," he spoke.

I sighed as I took a drink of my bourbon.

"I'm curious about this new hotel you're building in Vegas."

"Ah, the digital hotel. What about it? My father and I are very excited to break ground."

"It's a great idea. Where did you get it from?"

He stared at me while he picked up his drink and swirled the ice cubes in his glass.

"What is this really about, Gabriel?"

"You know what it's about!" I spoke through gritted teeth as I leaned across the table. "Building a hotel like that had been my father's dream for the past ten years."

"And?" he asked. "Do you think you're the only hotel chain that has thought of this? Let me ask you, Gabriel, why do you think your company is so special? Do you honestly think that you're the only one who wants to build hotels of the future? Many more companies will be jumping on this. Marriott, Hilton, Mandarin, Royals, Westin. They all will." He got up from his seat. "Competition is fierce, my friend, and we all do what we must to get to the top. I'm afraid I must go now." He started to walk away, but he turned and looked at me before he did. "By the way, how is your friend Kate doing? I thoroughly enjoyed our conversations in Hawaii. I was hoping to take her out sometime. Have her give me a call." He winked with a smile as he walked away.

I sat there, my blood pressure at an all-time high. I began to sweat with anger, and it took everything I had not to go after him and beat the shit out of him. When I got home, I pulled the article out and reread it. Marcel had explained what his hotel would consist of word for word, what I had told Kate.

"Fuck!" I threw the article on my desk.

~

K ate
    I decided to forget about Thaddeus and go straight to the source: Marcel. He was a slime-ball, and just by talking to him briefly in Hawaii, I already had a feel for how to handle him. I did as much research as I could. I found an interesting article published about six months ago in a magazine where he was interviewed as one of New York's most eligible bachelors.

Interviewer: "You're handsome and wealthy. I'm surprised you're still single. Do you like the bachelor life, or is it you just haven't found the right woman yet to settle down with?"

Marcel: "The bachelor life is good, and I'm enjoying it very much. Men like me need to be careful about the women we date. A lot of them are only interested in the money we have to offer. But I'm not giving up hope. I come from a background where family is very important, and I know the right woman is out there for me. I just haven't met her yet."

Interviewer: "Describe the perfect woman in your eyes."

Marcel: "She must be intelligent and family-oriented. She is well-educated and knows what she wants. She must have a good heart and a beautiful soul."

Interviewer: "How about on the outside? Is there a certain type of woman that catches your eye? Describe your dream girl."

Marcel: "If you're talking about looks, there is. Since I am six foot three, I am attracted to taller women, and I love long hair, preferably brunettes with deep green eyes—eyes that resemble an emerald. I like a woman who takes great pride in her looks and dresses."

Interviewer: "Well, I guess I can count myself out since I'm a redhead."

Marcel: "You're still a beautiful woman, and judging by that gorgeous diamond ring you're wearing on your left hand, you're also married."

Okay. He liked tall brunettes with dark green eyes. Perfect. The article also talked about his hobbies and how he liked to take his coffee: two creams and one teaspoon of sugar. Check. He loved children and wanted at least four. I shuddered at the thought. Maybe one or two, but for me, four was too many. He loved long walks, chess, and listening to classical music. Chess was good. I knew how to play, and I was good at it. My father loved to play and taught me. He always said chess was the perfect game to keep your mind sharp and always thinking. Strategy was the key, not only in the game but in life. Tomorrow, I would start the process.

Follow him, watch him, get him to notice me, and then start my deception. I needed to do this one last time, not only for Gabriel but for me. Once I found what I was looking for, it would be time to move on and start my life over.

Chapter Thirty-Four

Kate

I spent a week watching Marcel. I followed him to a diner in Harlem one afternoon. He walked in and took a seat, and I made sure I sat at a table behind him. He looked at me but didn't give me a second look. I wasn't his type, for I was dressed in ripped jeans, an oversized sweatshirt, and a pair of dirty tennis shoes, and I had on my short platinum wig with a pair of brown contacts in my eyes and a makeup-less face. I would admit that I wouldn't even give me a second look. I found it odd that he would choose this hole-in-the-wall diner in Harlem. It wasn't his style. He kept looking at the door as if waiting to meet someone. Holding the menu up, covering my face, I peered over it when the bell over the diner door chimed, and a man dressed in a navy-blue business suit walked in and took the seat across from him. A man whom I'd seen before. Thaddeus Wilson.

"You're late, Thaddeus," Marcel spoke as he looked at his watch.

"Sorry, but I was in a meeting that took longer than expected."

"What's with this secret lunch? I told you I would contact you once things were squared away," Marcel spoke.

"And it seems to be taking longer than expected. I gave you what you asked for six months ago, Marcel."

"I know, and I'm grateful. Patience, my friend. My lawyer is drawing up the paperwork as we speak. It should only be a matter of time."

"I hope so. I want to get to Paris as soon as possible."

"If we're done here," Marcel spoke, "I need to get going. I'm hosting a cocktail party at The Plaza Hotel at seven o'clock."

"We're done," Thaddeus spoke.

As Marcel walked out, Thaddeus ordered a cup of coffee and a slice of cherry pie. Paris? What did Marcel offer him in exchange for information? I needed to find out, and I would put my plan into motion tonight at The Plaza.

I sat there, my hands wrapped around the white coffee cup, staring at Thaddeus. His eyes diverted to me, and then quickly looked away. I made him uncomfortable. I could tell. He shifted in his seat as he looked at me again. He didn't like that the unattractive girl was staring at him. He reached inside his pocket, pulled out his wallet, and removed what looked like a business card. Placing his wallet back in his pocket, he picked up his phone and made a phone call. I looked over at my oversized black hobo-style purse and then back at him. The waitress walked over and placed his coffee and cherry pie down in front of him. After ending his call, he picked up his fork. I summoned the waitress for the bill and left some cash on the table. Picking up my purse and throwing it over my shoulder, I got up from my seat and intentionally dropped my phone by his table. I knew he wouldn't be a gentleman and pick it up for me since I was an eyesore to him. After dropping it on the floor, I bent down, and my bag swung across his table, knocking his coffee cup over.

"What the fuck!" he exclaimed as he pushed himself and his chair back.

"Oh my god! I am so sorry," I spoke as I looked up at him.

"You damn klutz!" he shouted.

The waitress hurried over with a towel as I got up and grabbed a shitload of napkins that were sitting on the table.

"Oh no. Your suit," I spoke as I patted his suitcoat with the napkins.

He grabbed them from my hand.

"Just go!" he shouted.

I pulled my wallet from my purse and threw down a hundred-dollar bill.

"This should cover your dry-cleaning bill and your coffee and pie. Accidents happen, sir, and you don't have to be so rude."

He looked at the hundred on the table and then up at me.

"I hope you have a better day." I walked away.

Once I hit the pavement and walked down the street, I reached into my purse and pulled out his black leather Bottega Veneta two-fold wallet with a smile. He was one man I didn't feel guilty ripping off. I counted six hundred fifty dollars to check out how much cash he had. Before returning to my apartment, I stopped at the salon and got a mani/pedi and a spray tan, compliments of Thaddeus Wilson.

When I got home, I pulled a black suitcase from the hall closet, took it to my room, and placed it on my bed. Opening it, I looked at all the face pieces I had used over the years—different noses, teeth, lips, and colored contacts. Walking over to my closet, I reached up and took down my long, wavy, brunette-colored wig with the subtle blonde highlights. After showering, I put on my face, popped the emerald-green-colored contacts into my eyes, and carefully pulled on my wig. I slipped into a black, off-the-shoulder, midi-length, form-fitted dress. It was very plain but elegant. Especially after I dressed it up with jewelry and black stiletto heels. When I purchased the dress, it was labeled "Lady Luck," and I needed luck tonight. Standing in the full-length mirror, I didn't even recognize myself. My nose was different, and my lips were fuller.

When I reached The Plaza, I wasn't sure which restaurant Marcel would be hosting his cocktail party. If I had to guess, and knowing him, it would be at the Palm Court. I was right because when I walked in, I saw him walking from table to table, mingling with guests. Luckily, there were a few seats still open at the round bar. Taking my seat, I asked the bartender for a cosmopolitan. I sat there for over an hour, watching him as he stole small glances my way. I had his attention and saw him start to walk my way.

"Are you here alone?" he asked with a smile as he approached me.

"I was supposed to be on a date, but I guess I got stood up," I replied with a French accent.

"You're French?" he asked with a hint of excitement.

"Oui." I smiled. "And so are you."

"Why on earth would anyone stand up a beautiful woman like yourself? His loss is my gain. May I?" His hand gestured to the stool next to me.

"You may." I smiled as I traced the rim of my glass.

Instantly, we hit it off. Or should I say, he did. We

talked about France, and I fabricated this story about how I was born in Marseille and how my parents moved to the United States when I was eight. He asked what I did for a living. I told him I was a freelance artist and worked from home. He seemed impressed. I mentioned that I wanted to start an online business. He told me he could help. I picked his brain for ideas and made him feel special. We talked about his company. I sat and listened, never breaking eye contact. He was hooked.

I looked at my watch. It was getting late. He ditched his cocktail party and spent the rest of the evening talking to me.

"I better get going. It's getting late." I smiled.

"I understand, but I'm afraid I can't let you leave without getting your phone number first."

"Hand me your phone." A smile crossed my lips as I held out my hand.

He pulled his phone from his pocket, handed it to me, and I put in my new number.

"There. Now you have my number. I will be expecting a call or text from you very soon." I grinned.

"Believe me, Camille, you will be hearing from me."

"Thank you for a wonderful evening and for making me forget that I was stood up."

"It was my pleasure. Can I take you home?"

I placed my hand on his chest.

"Thank you, but I can get home just fine. Have a good night, Marcel."

"You too."

I let out a deep breath as a smile crossed my lips, and I left The Plaza.

When I arrived home, I removed my shoes, went into the bathroom to remove my disguise, and climbed into bed.

As I lay there, the thoughts of Gabriel washed over me. The hurt and the pain I tried to bury crept up inside me. I had spent my entire life feeling lonely, but this was the loneliest I'd ever felt. As I closed my eyes, my phone dinged. I reached over and took it from my nightstand and saw a text message from Marcel.

"I can't stop thinking about you and would love to take you to dinner tomorrow evening."

"I would love to have dinner with you."

"Excellent. I can pick you up around seven o'clock."

"Name the restaurant, and I'll meet you there. I have a meeting with a client at six, but it won't take long."

"Very well. I'll text you the place and the address tomorrow. Good night, Camille."

"Good night, Marcel."

Now I had to figure out how to get out of sleeping with him because a man like him wouldn't be patient very long. I needed to find out the information I was looking for quickly. My time limit was one week. The faster I got this done, the sooner I could move.

The following day, I went out, bought a label gun, and made a new label with the name "Chamberlin" on it to replace my name under my apartment number outside the doors of the building. There was no use lying to Marcel about where I lived because once all was said and done, I'd be gone anyway.

～

Five Days Later

Things with Marcel were hitting an all-time high. He was in love with me and sent me a bouquet of fresh roses every day since the night we met. We spent every evening together, going on walks through Central Park, having dinner at the finest restaurants, and having drinks back at his penthouse while we played chess. My period. That was my excuse for not jumping into bed with him. On the first couple of dates, I explained that I wasn't that kind of girl and needed to know someone before I slept with them. He understood and respected me for it. Date three, I played it out as if I was ready. I even made the first move. As we were making out, and I was trying not to gag, I excused myself to the restroom, and when I came out, I told him that I had just started my period. I explained that it came out of nowhere and how bad it was, and I needed to go home. He was disappointed, but I promised to make it up to him. Date four was spent at my place, having dinner and talking for hours. I knew more than I wanted to about him. I didn't care. He repulsed me as much as I repulsed myself because what he did wasn't any different from everything I had done. This was my chance to make things right in my life. To make up for all the bad things I had done to the men I conned. To make things right for Gabriel. Even though we could never be what we once were, I couldn't stand by and let Marcel rip him off. Ultimately, doing this was the right thing for both of us.

Chapter Thirty-Five

Kate

Date five. The Friends of New Yorkers for Children Annual Ball was held at the Mandarin Oriental. The same hotel where Gabriel first saw me after we parted ways at JFK. I put on my face and wig and slipped into a Roland Mouret strapless two-tone peplum evening gown in cream and black. The gown was gorgeous with its double-face silk satin, asymmetric neckline, fitted bodice, and peplum waist. Compliments of Mr. Thaddeus Wilson and the one credit card he forgot to cancel.

"You look absolutely stunning." Marcel smiled and kissed my cheek.

"Thank you. So do you." I flashed my sexy smile.

He held my hand, led me to his limo, and we went to the ball. The Mandarin was filled with socialites. We mingled amongst the wealthy, and Marcel introduced me as his girlfriend. Shit was getting real, and I needed to move fast. Upon walking through the doors, we headed to the bar after having a glass of champagne, and Marcel ordered me a cosmopolitan. As I waited for my drink, I looked around the room, and my eyes locked with Gabriel's. Fuck! Fuck! Fuck! I didn't expect to see him here. My heart started racing, and suddenly, I became nervous. I needed to hold my composure, for I couldn't risk him finding out it was me. Shit. He'd know. As long as I didn't smile, I'd be okay, or so I thought. He walked away from the bar. I let out the deep breath I was holding. Marcel turned around and handed me my drink.

"One cosmopolitan for the most beautiful woman in the room." He smiled.

"Thank you."

He held out his arm, and I placed mine around it as we walked to our table and took a seat. As I sipped my cosmopolitan, Gabriel sat down across from us.

"Looks like we're table mates," he spoke to Marcel.

"Ah, very good. Gabriel, I'd like you to meet my girl-friend, Camille Chamberlin. Camille, this is a friend of mine, Gabriel Quinn. He's the CEO of Quinn Hotels."

Shit. Shit. Shit. I could do this.

"Nice to meet you, Gabriel," I spoke without a smile in my French accent as I extended my hand.

Placing his hand in mine, he looked down and then back up at me. His eyes told me he felt something.

"The pleasure is all mine, Camille." He brought my hand up to his lips.

Jerk. Does he always kiss the hand of a female he meets for the first time?

I pulled my hand away and set it on my lap. The sensation that ripped through my body as his lips touched me was too much. All the while he and Marcel talked, he kept looking at me. He was alone, which made me happy because I didn't think I could bear to see him with another woman. He turned his attention to me and began asking me all sorts of questions. Fuck. He was suspicious. I could see it in his eyes.

~

G abriel

Marcel's girlfriend was beautiful. Too beautiful for the likes of him. Something about her wasn't sitting right with me. I couldn't put my finger on it. A jolt of lightning soared through me the moment I touched her hand. Just like—I began to ask her questions, hoping she'd slip up somehow, and I'd know for sure. Thaddeus walked over and took the seat next to mine. Marcel introduced Camille to him. I waited for her to smile. She wouldn't because she knew if she did, I would know for sure it was her. Fuck. I felt it. There was definitely a strong connection when I touched her. I swallowed hard at the thought. There had only been one woman in my life I felt that connection with, and it was with Kate. I kept an eye on her during dinner, and she quickly looked away every time I looked at her.

Music started to play, a variety of jazz and blues. The dance floor opened, and Marcel took Camille by the hand and escorted her to the middle of the ballroom. I leaned back in my chair and watched them while sipping my drink.

"Damn. Marcel's girlfriend is fucking hot," Thaddeus spoke.

"She certainly is beautiful."

"Beautiful and French. What more could a man ask for." He smirked.

It was the middle of the song, so I finished my drink and headed to the dance floor.

"May I cut in?" I asked Marcel.

"Of course." He nodded.

I wrapped one arm around her waist and held her other hand in mine. She stared over my shoulder.

"You're a very beautiful woman, Camille."

"Thank you," she spoke.

"Too beautiful for the likes of Marcel."

A small smile crossed her plump lips but quickly disappeared once she realized what she had done. It was Kate. My grip around her waist tightened as I pulled her closer to me.

"What the hell are you doing, Kate?" I whispered in a stern voice.

Not a word escaped her mouth.

"I asked you a question. Do you want me to cause a scene? Because I fucking will, and then when Marcel comes to your rescue, I'll flatten his scrawny ass right here in front of everyone."

"Really, Gabriel?" she whispered in her normal voice. "Two respectable CEOs going at it in the middle of a fundraiser for children. The press would have a field day."

"I'll ask you one last time. What are you doing with him? Was this your plan all along? Were the two of you in cahoots before we even met?"

"Oh my god, no!" she voiced loudly.

"Shh. Keep it down. Do you want to draw attention to us?"

"Leave me alone, Gabriel. I have a job to do."

"A job? What are you ripping off from him? Oh, wait. That would be my ideas and plans for the hotel."

Tears started to form in her eyes.

"You're wrong."

"Am I, Kate? Because I don't think I am." The song ended, and I let go of her. "I wish I'd never met you. You are nothing but a vile human being." I shook my head as I walked away.

Chapter Thirty-Six

Kate

I gulped as I stood there, trying to hold back the tears in my eyes.

"Are you okay, darling?" Marcel asked as he walked over to me.

"Of course." I smiled. "I'm fine. Just a little lightheaded from the champagne and cosmos."

"Would you like to go home?"

"I think that's a good idea. I really need to lie down."

He walked me up to my apartment, and before I opened the door, I told him good night.

"Thank you for a beautiful evening, Marcel. I had a lot of fun."

"You're welcome, my dear." He stroked my chin with his thumb. "I wish that period of yours would end."

"Me too. It should only be a couple of more days." I brushed my lips against his.

"What are your plans for tomorrow?" he asked.

"I was hoping to spend the day with you since it's Saturday."

"Then your wish is my command. What shall we do?"

"It's supposed to rain all day, so I thought we could just spend the day at your place. I could cook for you, and we could relax and watch movies." I smiled.

"I would love that. I haven't had a relaxing day in months."

"Great. I'll stop at the store, pick up everything I need, and head over around noon."

"Maybe you could spend the night with me." His lips touched mine.

"We'll see. Good night, Marcel. I really do need to lie down."

"Good night, Camille." He kissed me one last time.

I stepped inside my apartment and shut the door. I took in a deep breath as I placed my hands on the island. Tomorrow had to be the day that would end all of this. I wanted to tell Gabriel what I was doing but couldn't. Without the physical proof I needed, I couldn't risk him going after Marcel and Thaddeus.

The following day, as I was getting ready to leave, the buzzer to my apartment rang. Shit.

"Yes?" I spoke over the intercom.

"Let me in, Kate!" Caleb sternly spoke.

Rolling my eyes, I buzzed him and opened the door.

"What the hell are you doing?" he spoke as he entered my apartment. "Oh, my God. Look at you. What the fuck, Kate?"

"I'm guessing you spoke to your brother."

"Yeah. We had breakfast this morning, and I couldn't believe what he told me. I specifically told you not to do this."

"No. You said not to do this with Thaddeus."

"You're crazy." He threw his hands up in the air.

"Listen to me, Caleb. You were right about Thaddeus. He was the one who told Marcel about the plans for the hotel, and if I'm right, he also copied the blueprint and gave it to him. I will find out everything today and get the proof I need to clear me."

"Jesus. How do you know all this?"

"I followed Marcel to a diner in Harlem, where he met with Thaddeus. I was sitting at a table behind them, and I heard everything. Marcel offered him some position in his company in Paris in exchange for the information about the hotel."

"How are you going to get the proof?"

"I have a plan. Don't worry about me. How's Gabriel?"

"How do you think he is? He's angry and hurt. He barely ate. I've never seen him like this. He's torn up inside as it is, and now that he thinks you were involved with Marcel the whole time, it's killing him."

"You didn't tell him what I was doing, did you?"

"No. How the hell could I? I didn't even know. Kate," he took hold of my arm, "you have to be careful."

"I will. Never underestimate the charm of a beautiful woman." I smirked. "I have to go. I'm spending the day with Marcel, and I have to stop at the store first."

"I hope this works." He shook his head.

"It will. Please don't say a word about this to Gabriel."

I stopped at the store and picked up everything I needed to make a nice dinner for us. He immediately took the bags from my arms when I reached his penthouse.

"I wish you would have called me from the lobby. I would have brought these up for you," he spoke as he kissed my lips.

"You're sweet, but I managed just fine."

He took the groceries into the kitchen. Just as the

weatherman predicted, it rained all day long. The sky was overcast, and the slight chill in the air made it a perfect day to sit in the comfort of a home by the fire, keeping warm while watching TV. We snuggled on the couch under a blanket, watched a movie, and talked. I was ready to talk about Gabriel and get this fucking night over with, so I reached into the pocket of the oversized hoodie I was wearing and pressed the play button on the recorder I had hidden in my pocket.

"That man from last night. Gabriel Quinn," I spoke.

"What about him?"

"Is he a major competitor for you?"

"You've never heard of him or his hotel chain?" he asked with a bewildered look.

"Vaguely," I replied. "Honestly, I don't really keep up with the hotel scene." I smiled.

"Ah. I see. Well, to answer your question, yes, he is a major competitor. Quinn Hotels always has been. But that is all going to change very soon."

"Really? How?"

"It's a secret, Camille, and one I can't discuss."

I sat up with a distraught look on my face as I stared at him.

"I thought you and I were a thing? I mean, you did introduce me as your girlfriend."

"We are. But business is something I cannot discuss."

"You can't, or you won't?" I spoke with an upset tone to my voice.

"Darling, why are you getting so upset?" His hand stroked my cheek.

"I'm not." I turned away from him. "It's just—"

"Just what?" His hand gripped my shoulder.

The words I had to speak made me nauseous.

"It's just that I love you, but I can't be involved with someone who keeps secrets from me. Business or personal."

"What? You love me?" he spoke in a soft voice.

Here we go—time to up my acting skills. I turned and faced him as I placed my hand on his cheek.

"Yes. I know it sounds crazy, Marcel, because we haven't known each other but for a very short time. I can't explain it. All I know is that I'm in love with you. This past week has been the best week of my life."

"Oh, darling." He smiled. "I love you too. I was smitten from the day my eyes laid sight on you."

"If you loved me, you wouldn't keep secrets from me." I pouted.

"I don't want to keep secrets from you."

"Marcel, I want a relationship with you but need total honesty. I love hearing about your business. The excitement your eyes show whenever you talk about it turns me on."

"How much does it turn you on?" he whispered as his tongue traveled across my neck.

I shuddered, and not in a good way.

"So much. Now tell me how you are knocking the competition right out."

"I stole the digital hotel idea from him. Actually, it was given to me by a friend and co-worker of his. You met him last night. Thaddeus Wilson."

"Oh. Scandalous. Tell me more." I began to unbutton his shirt.

"I made him an offer he couldn't refuse, and he handed the plans right over to me. I gave them to my people, and now, we're building it."

"You're such a badass." I smiled. "This calls for a celebration. You sit here while I pour us a glass of the wine I brought."

"I can do it, darling."

"No. No." I placed my hand on his hard cock. "You stay right here and let me, your girlfriend, serve you," I spoke in a seductive French accent.

"If you insist." He grinned.

I entered the kitchen, placed the recorder in my purse, and took out the bottle of sleeping pills I had brought. After opening the wine, I poured some into a glass, took out three sleeping pills, opened the capsules, and poured the powder into his wine. I poured my glass, walked to the living room, and handed him his.

"To your new hotel." I smiled as I held up my glass to him.

"Thank you, darling." He tapped his glass against mine and took a sip.

"The first person to finish their wine gets a special prize." I grinned.

"And what would that prize be?"

"If you finish your wine first, I'll give you a blow job. If I finish my wine first, you have to cook dinner."

"You aren't serious," he spoke.

"Oh, I'm very serious." I smiled as I licked my lips.

"Bottoms up!" He threw back his wine as if it was water.

Now, I needed those pills to work their magic as quickly as possible.

"Look at that. It seems I finished my wine first. Bring that beautiful mouth of yours down here."

A sick feeling washed over me. I needed to stall as long as I could. Getting down on my knees before him, I brushed my lips against his softly and teasingly. A growl erupted from his throat. I slid my fingers down his shirt until they reached his belt. Taking in a deep breath, I slowly unbuckled it. The bulge in his pants grew more prominent as I undid his pants. Looking up at him, I saw his head was tilted back, and his eyes were closed. As I stroked his hard cock through the fabric of his red silk underwear, he began to snore. Thank God! I quickly stood up, laid him down on the couch, and covered him with a blanket.

"Sorry, Marcel. Sweet dreams."

I took the wine glasses into the kitchen, washed and dried them, and then went into his office and sat down behind his desk. I opened his laptop, and the lock screen appeared.

"Shit. What would his password be?"

I opened his desk drawer, looking for something to indicate his password. Nothing. Damn it. I needed to do this quickly. I shut his laptop and walked back out to the living room, where I took his phone from the table and placed his finger on the button to unlock it. Pulling up his email, I searched it and found a folder labeled "Digital Hotel." I opened it and found a shitload of email exchanges between him and Thaddeus. After sending the folder to my email address, I deleted it in the sent file, set his phone back on the coffee table, grabbed my purse, and headed out the door.

After hailing a cab back to my apartment, I called a messenger service to deliver the recorder to Gabriel. Pulling out his business card that I had taken from his desk drawer a while back, I opened my laptop, created a new email address, and sent the folder from that one to his. I took the two suitcases I had packed from the closet and my guitar case and climbed into the cab waiting for me at the curb.

"Where to, miss?" the cab driver asked.

"Train station."

Before I launched my plan on Marcel, I visited my father and told him everything that had happened. He understood why I had to leave, but I promised to visit him as much as possible. Before we said our goodbyes, he slipped me a piece of paper with the number to a safe deposit box, which was in my name, at the Atlantic Bank.

"The box is in your name, baby girl. Take what's in there and go," he whispered with tears in his eyes. "Light up, sweet girl." He smiled.

I sat on the train for the four-hour ride to Mystic, Connecticut, which is classified as a village with a population of 4,025 people. Small. The perfect place to start new until I figured out exactly where I wanted to be in life. I walked from the train station to the Mermaid Inn of Mystic, a cute bed and breakfast that I found fitting.

"Hello, dear. How may I help you?" the older gray-haired woman behind the desk asked.

"Hi, I have a reservation."

"You must be Kate Harper." She smiled.

"How did you know?"

"You are our only guest, my dear. Everyone else already checked out. It's our slow time of the season. My name is Rose." She held out her slender hand.

"It's nice to meet you, Rose." A smile crossed my lips.

"When you called to book the reservation, you said you didn't know how long you'd need the room for. Have you decided yet?"

"Maybe a week or two."

"Delightful. I'll put you down for at least two weeks. Now follow me, and I'll show you to your room on the second floor. You can leave your suitcases down here, and my grandson, Thomas, will bring them up."

I followed her up the stairs to the second floor. She inserted the key in the lock and opened the door to the room.

"This is our Rose room. Named after me." She smiled. "I decorated it myself. I hope it meets your needs."

Walking into the room, I set my guitar case down and looked around. It was beautiful. The walls were painted a rose color and then stenciled with floral designs. A queen-size bed that housed a quaint floral print comforter sat on the far wall. A small dresser with a TV was mounted on the wall above it. It was very charming.

"There's a mini fridge over in that corner that is fully stocked with water and soft drinks, compliments of the inn."

"Thank you."

"There are towels in the cabinet over there outside the bathroom. If you need more, just let me know. Also, breakfast is served at nine a.m., so make sure you bring your appetite because we serve a full American breakfast."

"I definitely will." I smiled.

"I'll let you get settled, dear. If you have any questions about Mystic, ask."

As soon as Rose left the room, I walked over to the window and took in the view of the garden. I felt a sense of peace here. It was quiet and exactly what I needed. I grabbed a bottle of water from the refrigerator and took it to the gazebo surrounded by beautiful flowers.

Chapter Thirty-Seven

Gabriel

I was sitting in my office at home catching up on some work when the doorbell rang. A few moments later, Grace walked in and handed me a small package.

"This just came for you from a messenger service," she spoke.

I took the package from her and opened it. Pulling out what looked like a recording device, I studied it.

"What the hell is this?"

"Maybe it's something you need to listen to."

I pressed the play button and froze when I heard Kate's and Marcel's voices.

"Damn, she's good," Grace spoke.

A fire erupted inside me, and the air I breathed became restricted.

"Gabriel, calm down."

"Calm down?" I shouted. "You heard what was on that tape."

Sandi Lynn

I got up from my chair and threw the paperweight on my desk against the wall.

"Thaddeus." I shook my head in disbelief. "I'm going to kill him, and when I'm done, I'm going after Marcel."

Suddenly, the fact that Kate had nothing to do with it invaded my head.

"Oh, my God, what have I done," I slowly spoke as I gripped the arms of the chair and sat back down.

"She was telling the truth, Gabriel, and she went to great lengths to prove it to you," Grace spoke.

A sick feeling arose in the pit of my stomach. A sickness I'd never felt before. What I did was unforgivable. Suddenly, an email popped up on my computer. I opened it and found a file that contained emails between Marcel and Thaddeus. Emails with copies of my blueprints, data information, and every plan made for the hotel. I studied the email address: amermaidssong@yahoo.com.

"I need to go see her," I spoke as I rose from my chair.

"I'm not so sure she's going to want to see you after what you said to her."

"I'll make her see me. I have to apologize."

"It'll be a miracle if that girl ever forgives you for what you've said and done."

I shot her a look.

"I'm sorry, Gabriel, but it's the truth."

"Well, I have to try."

I flew out of the house and hailed a cab to her apartment. I didn't have time to wait for Carl. When I pressed the button for her apartment, I noticed the space where her name had sat was blank, as she no longer resided there. Someone was walking out of the building, and as soon as the door opened, I held it open for her and slipped inside.

Taking the elevator up to her apartment, I stood before it and knocked on the door. She didn't answer, so I knocked harder.

"Kate, it's me. Open up. We need to talk." I continued to pound on the door.

A woman walked down the hall and stopped at the apartment next to Kate's.

"If you're looking for the woman who lived there, she's gone," she spoke.

"Gone? What do you mean she's gone?"

"I think she moved out. Took her guitar and a couple of suitcases and left. I asked her if she was going on vacation, and she said no, she was leaving New York City for good."

"Did she say where she was going?"

"No. I didn't feel it was appropriate to ask since I'd never spoken to her before."

"Thank you." I walked past her and stepped onto the elevator.

Once I got inside the cab, I pulled my phone out and called Caleb.

"Hey, Gabriel, what's up?"

"I need you to come over as soon as possible. I need to talk to you. I was wrong about Kate, and now she's gone."

"What? Where is she?"

"I don't know. I'll explain everything when you get to the house."

"I'm on my way, bro."

Caleb pulled up behind me as I stepped out of the cab.

"What do you mean you were wrong about her?" he asked.

"She wasn't the one who told Marcel about the plans for the hotel."

"Oh, now you believe her?" he spoke with a snide tone.

As soon as we stepped inside the house, I grabbed the recorder and played it for Caleb.

"I can't believe she actually did it," he spoke as he slowly shook his head.

"What did you say?" I looked at him. "Did you know about this?"

"After breakfast, I went to her apartment, and she was just leaving for Marcel's place. She said she had a plan, and I told her not to do it. That it was too risky."

"Why didn't you tell me!" I shouted at him.

"Because you already decided that she was guilty, and you told her she was a vile human being. I honestly didn't think she would get Marcel to confess."

"She's Kate Harper. Have you forgotten? Damn it, Caleb! I can't believe you didn't tell me."

"She told me not to, and if I had, you would have gone after her and blown her cover. Just forget about Kate for a minute. What are you going to do about Thaddeus and Marcel?"

"I'm calling my lawyer right now." I pulled my phone from my pocket and shook my head at him.

I tossed and turned all night, thinking about Kate. I no longer cared about the hotel. None of that mattered to me anymore. I fucked up so badly that I was afraid Grace was right. Kate would never be able to forgive me for the things I said to her. I had to try, and I needed to find her. I would bet the one person who would know where she went would be her father.

I had Carl drive me to Rikers Island, where I cleared security and waited in the visiting room for Henry.

"May I help you?" he asked as he entered the room.

"Henry, I'm Gabriel Quinn."

A look of dismay and disapproval filled his eyes.

"I'm not a fan of yours, Mr. Quinn," he spoke.

"I'm sure Kate told you everything."

"She did." He nodded as he took a seat at the rectangular table.

"I need to know where she is. It's important."

"You hurt my baby girl in the worst way possible. I wouldn't tell you even if I knew where she was."

"Are you saying you don't know where she is?"

"That's right. She wouldn't tell me where she was going. She's trying to put the pieces of her life back together, Mr. Quinn, and you're not a part of that. In fact, you're the reason my little girl left in the first place. If you trusted her, you wouldn't be sitting across from me right now."

I wanted to shout obscenities at him and tell him what a lousy father he was, but I remained calm and let him say what he had to.

"I was wrong and need to make things right with her."

"I'm afraid it's too late for that."

"People deserve a second chance, Henry."

"You're right. They do. You should have thought about that before saying what you did to Kate. She's a very strong woman who knows how to care for herself. Look at the risk she took to prove her innocence to you. Move on with your life, Mr. Quinn." He got up from his seat, "And forget about Kate."

"I'm afraid I can't do that. I love her. I'm in love with her."

"If that's true and you really love her, then you must let her go. Let her find her way and get back on track with her life. I have. I'm not perfect and may not have been the best father, but I did what I could to support her."

"By moving her around her whole life and exposing her to your cons?" I spoke.

"I regret that, but I couldn't let them take her away from me. She was all I had left in this world after her mother died."

"You couldn't let who take her away from you?"

"Her grandparents. They always hated me and threatened to take her away because they thought I couldn't support her. They told me that I'd be better off giving her up to them because a loser and a con like me could never love or take care of her the way they could. I did what I had to do to keep her."

"Does Kate know any of this?" I asked.

"No. I never told her. Have a good day, Mr. Quinn."

He walked to the door, summoned the guard, and left. As I was leaving, my phone rang, and it was Giles, my attorney.

"Giles," I answered.

"I wanted to let you know that Thaddeus and Marcel are under investigation by the feds, and the press is having a field day with this. The judge ordered a restraint on Marcel's building of the hotel until the investigation is completed. It's up to you to get Thaddeus arrested for theft and espionage."

"Yes. I want him to pay for what he did."

"Very well. I'll be in touch, my friend."

I sighed as I climbed into the limo and headed home. I poured myself a drink and paced around the room, trying to figure out where the hell she could have gone.

"Did she ever mention somewhere she'd like to go?" Grace asked as she saw me in deep thought.

"Not that I can recall."

"Why don't you hire a private investigator to find her?"

"I'll have to because I need to talk to her. Even if she doesn't forgive me, I need to apologize."

Chapter Thirty-Eight

Kate

Rose and her husband, Bobby, were wonderful people. They made me feel so welcome in the two days I had already been there. I spent an entire day exploring downtown Mystic, meeting the people there, and shopping in the cute little boutiques they had to offer. It kept my mind off Gabriel, at least for a while. The hurt hadn't even begun to lessen, and my heart was still shattered into tiny pieces. My first heartbreak ever, and I had no clue how to heal from it.

The gazebo had become my favorite spot to sit in and reflect on my life. As I sat there, staring at the beautiful garden, Rose came along and sat beside me.

"How are you liking Mystic so far?"

"I love it here. This place is exactly what I needed."

She placed her hand on top of mine and gave it a gentle squeeze.

"What brought you to Mystic? Somehow, I feel you're running from someone or something."

"How did you know?"

"I can tell these things."

"I'm running from my life." I gave her a small smile. "I've done some terrible things and want to start over. It's never too late for that, right?"

"Of course not, dear. That's how we, as human beings grow. We make mistakes, learn from them, and then move on."

"Can I ask you something, Rose?"

"Of course, you can."

"How long does it take for a broken heart to heal?"

"Well, it depends on the person. This isn't your first broken heart, is it?"

I looked down as I clasped my hands.

"It is. I've never let myself get close enough to anyone before. I always played by my own rules. Then, I met this man, and as hard as I tried to shield myself from him, I couldn't. I fell in love when I knew deep in my mind that he could never trust me."

"Why's that?" she asked.

"Because of the way we met. That's another story all on its own. Something happened with his company, and instantly, he accused me. He didn't believe me even though I told him I didn't do it. He said horrible things and told me he never wanted to see me again. My life was normal when I was with him—a normalcy I craved my entire life." A tear ran down my cheek.

Rose wrapped her arm around me and pulled me into her. Even though I had only known her for a couple of days, I felt like she was a mother figure—something I'd never had.

"It's okay to cry, Kate. Getting over a broken heart and relationship is something that takes time. Time will and does heal all wounds."

"I never should have let myself get involved with him."

"Of course, you should have because then you never would have experienced the love you felt for him."

"The pain. This pain isn't worth it. It hurts so much." I began to cry. "I just want it to stop."

"And it will, dear, but you are the only one who can heal yourself. Isn't that why you came here?"

"Yes."

"Then you've already taken the first step. Just keep going. The pain will lessen every day until you wake up, and it won't hurt anymore."

"Thanks, Rose." I gently smiled.

"You're welcome, dear. I'm going to go start dinner. Would you like to help?"

"I'd love to."

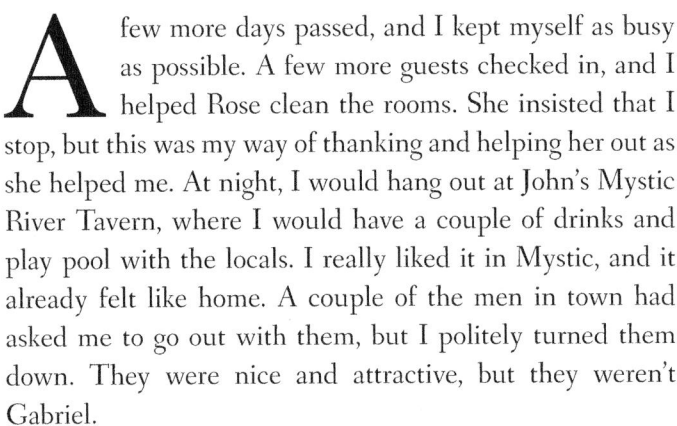

A few more days passed, and I kept myself as busy as possible. A few more guests checked in, and I helped Rose clean the rooms. She insisted that I stop, but this was my way of thanking and helping her out as she helped me. At night, I would hang out at John's Mystic River Tavern, where I would have a couple of drinks and play pool with the locals. I really liked it in Mystic, and it already felt like home. A couple of the men in town had asked me to go out with them, but I politely turned them down. They were nice and attractive, but they weren't Gabriel.

Gabriel

I spent days trying to figure out where the hell Kate went off to. It was affecting my work. I couldn't stay focused, and I didn't care. Work was no longer my number one priority. Finding Kate was. I had just arrived home from the office and walked up to the bedroom where she stayed. Sitting down on the bed, I cupped my face in my hands. The best thing that ever happened to me in my life, and I threw it away for nothing. I never should have accused her. I should have believed her when she told me she wasn't the one who told Marcel about the hotel because I loved her. I sighed as I ran my hands down my face. When I looked up, I stared at the painting of the mermaid by the sea she painted. It was beautiful, just like her. Suddenly, something hit me and hit me hard. I jumped up from the bed and ran down the stairs to my office. Opening my laptop, I typed the word mermaid into the search bar. I scrolled and scrolled, looking for something, anything that would lead me to where she was. What was I doing? I laughed at myself for even thinking I would find something. I went to shut my laptop, and something caught my attention. The Mermaid Inn of Mystic—a bed and breakfast in Mystic, Connecticut. Could she have gone there? Or was I grasping at straws? I shook my head as I closed my laptop, poured myself a bourbon, and went up to bed.

~

I tossed and turned all night like I did every night after I kicked Kate out. I stumbled out of bed. As I was showering, I couldn't stop thinking about The Mermaid Inn. It was a long shot, but I didn't care. The drive was only two and a half hours and something I needed to do. I got dressed, packed a small bag, and headed out the door.

I reached the bed and breakfast, walked through the door, and found an older woman behind the desk.

"Welcome to The Mermaid Inn." She smiled.

"Thank you. I'm hoping you can help me. I'm looking for someone."

"I can try to be of some help," she spoke.

"I'm looking for a woman who's about five foot seven, with long blonde hair and beautiful blue eyes. Her name is Kate Harper. She would have stayed here within the past week."

"No, I'm sorry. No one by that name or description has stayed here."

"Do you know everyone who stays here?" I asked.

"Of course. There are only four rooms available at my bed and breakfast. I know every guest that walks through that door."

"It was a long shot. Thank you. Do you, by chance, have any rooms available for tonight?"

"Unfortunately, every room is booked right now."

"I see. Have a good day," I spoke.

"You too."

I climbed into the car and followed the sign that pointed to Downtown Mystic. I was here, and it seemed nice, so I decided to stay the night. Maybe getting away, even for a night, would do me some good. I pulled into The Whaler's Inn to see if they had any rooms. Luckily for me, they had their junior suite available.

"We hope you enjoy your stay, Mr. Quinn."

"Thank you. I'm sure I will."

I set my bag on the bed and looked around the nautical-themed room. Pulling my phone from my pocket, I called Caleb.

"Hey, bro," he answered.

"Hey. I just wanted you to know that I'm in Mystic, Connecticut. I'll be staying a couple of days and turning my phone off."

"Why are you in Mystic?" he asked with a surprised tone.

"There was this inn called The Mermaid Inn of Mystic. I thought maybe Kate would be there, but the owner said she wasn't. It's pretty nice here, and I need a couple of days to myself."

"I get it. Okay. Try to relax while you're there."

"I'll call you when I get back to New York."

"Talk to you soon, Gabriel."

I turned off my phone and placed it in my pocket. Maybe a change of scenery would help get Kate off my mind. I took a stroll through the downtown area, grabbed some dinner, and returned to the hotel for the night. As I walked up the stairs to my room, I saw a young couple holding hands and smiling at each other as they talked. It hit a spot in my heart because that was what Kate and I used to do. I saw the same look in that woman's eyes that Kate always had when she smiled. Fuck. I wasn't supposed to be thinking about her.

The next morning, I got up early and ran along the river. It was a chilly start to the day, but the weather was perfect for running. I ran for what seemed like miles, trying to escape all my problems. I needed a clear head before I headed back to New York, but I wasn't so sure that would happen. As I ran back to the hotel, I saw a woman standing outside a boutique, looking in the window: her hair, height, and body frame. My heart started pounding. It was Kate. I ran towards her and placed my hand on her shoulder as I approached.

"Kate, thank God I found you."

She turned around, and instantly, I froze. It wasn't her.

"Excuse me?" she spoke.

"I'm so sorry. I thought you were someone else. I'm sorry." I continued my run to the hotel.

Now I had gone and completely lost it, thinking that every woman I saw with long blonde hair was her. After breakfast, I decided to head back to New York, but first, I needed to stop at a small boutique I had passed yesterday. Grace collected crystal birds, and I saw a unique one displayed in the window. Her birthday was coming up, and I thought it would be a little something extra to give along with a bonus. After making the purchase, I stopped at a small coffee house to have a cup of coffee before heading home.

"How may I help you?" the young barista asked.

"I'll have a medium coffee and a scone," I replied.

"Will that be for here or to go?"

"To go. On second thought, for here."

The last time I drove while drinking a cup of coffee, I spilled it all over me and the car. I sat at a small table with my back to the door to view the river one last time before I left. As I was drinking my coffee, I heard a woman's voice. A voice that made my heart start to race. I slowly turned around and saw Kate standing at the counter, talking to the barista. She grabbed her coffee and headed out the door. I quickly got up and followed her, staying far behind so she didn't see me. I wasn't quite sure how to approach her, and I was nervous. She was just as beautiful as she always was, and seeing her again took my breath away like it had many times before.

I followed her to The Mermaid Inn. What the hell? Had she been there the whole time, and that woman lied to me? I waited outside the bed and breakfast while she went inside. After a few moments, I walked through the door and saw the older woman behind the desk.

"You lied to me," I spoke as I approached her.

"Excuse me?" Her brow arched.

"The woman who just walked through the door, that was Kate. The woman I asked you about yesterday."

"I think you should leave, Mr. Quinn. Kate came here to heal a broken heart."

"And I came here looking for her to make things right."

"Gabriel?" I heard Kate's voice on the stairs.

I looked over at her and saw the sadness that resided in her eyes.

"What are you doing here?" she asked.

"I came looking for you." I smiled as I walked towards her.

"You shouldn't have."

She quickly walked past me and out the door. I ran after her.

"Kate, I need you to listen to me. Please."

"Go back to New York, Gabriel." She continued walking at a rapid pace.

"I'm not leaving until I apologize to you. I'm sorry for everything I've said and done."

"Fine. I accept, now go. Leave me alone!" she shouted.

I caught up with her and lightly grabbed hold of her arm. She turned, and her beautiful blue eyes stared into mine.

"I'm so sorry. Please, let's go somewhere so we can talk in private."

"There's nothing to talk about. You said everything you

needed to back when you accused me of selling you out to Marcel." She jerked her arm away.

"Please, sweetheart. I need you to listen to me."

"First of all," she pointed her finger at me and spoke angrily, "I'm not your sweetheart, and second of all, I don't care if you need me to listen to you. You didn't listen to me. All of this could have been avoided if you had just believed in me!"

"I know that, and I'm sorry. I was stupid and turned my back on the only woman I had ever loved. I'm here to make things right. I can't eat, I can't sleep, and I can't focus on my company. What I did was wrong, and I made a terrible mistake. I'm so sorry, Kate. Please, you have to believe me."

"Just like you believed me?" she asked in a low and sad voice. "I accept your apology, but that's all I can give you. Gabriel, things are different now, and you must go home."

"Kate, please. I need you." I reached out and grabbed her hand.

"And I needed you at one time, and you turned your back on me." She pulled her hand away. "Goodbye, Gabriel. Please just leave me alone." Tears formed in her eyes. "You will never be able to trust me." She walked away and headed back to the bed and breakfast.

"You're wrong, Kate," I shouted.

I stood there and watched her walk away from me. The pain I already felt intensified to something so unbearable it sent me to my knees. My eyes began to water. Before I knew it, tears started streaming down my face. This wasn't me. This wasn't who I was. She changed me. Now, I'd never know what it would be like to love her and spend my life with her.

Chapter Thirty-Nine

Kate

I ran back to the Inn and found Rose standing on the porch. The uncontrollable tears streamed down my face as I cried in her arms.

"There, there, dear. It'll be okay," she whispered as she held the back of my head with her hand.

As soon as I calmed down, she walked me over to the gazebo, where we always had our little talks. Seeing him again hurt so much. The fact that he searched and found me led me to believe he really was sorry for everything he'd done. But it didn't matter. I needed to move on with my life because I would never allow myself to go through this again with him. People always say the way you meet someone is the way things will end. We met under non-trust circumstances, and we ended the same way. Rose and I sat and talked for hours.

"Everybody deserves a second chance at least one time in their life," she spoke. "Things with Bobby and me weren't always so good."

"But you two have a perfect relationship."

"We do now because of second chances. Bobby made a mistake in the early years and cheated on me."

I looked at her as shock splayed across my face.

"I'd just had my third miscarriage. We were both devastated because we thought for sure it wouldn't happen again. I went into a deeper depression and shut him out completely. He tried so hard to be there for me, but I wouldn't let him. I failed to recognize that he was hurting just as badly as I was. I wasn't there to ease his pain like he was for me. I could only focus on how much these miscarriages affected me. I never thought about how it affected him. He went out one night after we fought, got drunk, and slept with a woman he met at the bar."

"Rose, I'm so sorry."

"I'm not. Because if he didn't, we wouldn't be together today."

"How could you trust him again after that?"

"It took a while and months of therapy. But I knew he loved me more than anything in the world, and I loved him. After that horrible time and pain we went through, we found each other again, and our relationship was better than ever. I gave him a second chance because he deserved to be given one. And he gave me one because he loved me. Later that year, I got pregnant and had my son, Gage. When he was six months old, I got pregnant again and had my daughter, Kathryn. Those two children never would have been born if I had given up on him."

"I appreciate your story, Rose, but I'm not having children. At least not for a few years, if ever."

"It isn't always about the children, Kate. It's about your life and the wonderful things you could miss out on because you're letting your pain and heartache decide your future."

I sighed as I laid my head on her shoulder.

"Running away doesn't solve anything. You have a home in New York, and your father is there. Do you want to miss out on time spent with him because of Gabriel?"

"I can't be in the same city as him. It would hurt too much."

"You just think you can't. You're a strong woman, Kate Harper, and you can get through this. First heartbreaks are always the hardest, but it doesn't mean you must run away from your life and home to heal. You can make a fresh start in New York. Change your routine and habits. Before you know it, your life will be exactly how you envisioned it. Besides, I'm only a two-and-a-half-hour drive away, and I'll always have a room ready and waiting for you when you need it. You are welcome here anytime and as much as you want to be here."

"Thanks, Rose. I love you."

"I love you too, dear."

I took everything Rose said to heart and decided I needed to return to New York to live my life. I liked it there, and my father was only a short distance away. I packed my bags the following day, and Rose walked with me to the train station.

"Goodbye, my darling Kate." She smiled as she placed her hands on my face. "Have a safe trip home. Please call me or text when you get there."

A smile crossed my lips. "I will, and I promise to keep in touch."

"You better because I consider you a daughter, and I'll worry."

~

G abriel
I couldn't bring myself to drive home after Kate and I had words, so I spent the rest of the day sitting by the river, thinking back on our conversation. She hated me, and I didn't blame her. I was foolish to think that the minute she saw me, she'd run into my arms and tell me she forgave me. She said she forgave me, but I knew deep down she only said that to make me leave.

The next morning, I checked out of the hotel and drove to the bed and breakfast to see her one last time. I didn't come to try and get her back because I knew she didn't want that. I just needed to see her one last time for closure because I'd never see her again after today. She wanted that, and I would respect her wishes no matter how bad it killed me inside.

I walked through the door and found the older woman dusting the coffee table in the living area.

"Hello," I nervously spoke.

She turned, and a small smile swept over her lips when she looked at me.

"Mr. Quinn, I thought you went home."

"I'm on my way now but need to see Kate again. Can you tell me which room she's staying in?"

"I'm afraid she's left already."

"What? Where did she go?"

"Look at that." She looked over at the clock that hung on the wall. "It's lunchtime." She smiled. "I think it would be in your best interest to join me. You shouldn't drive home on an empty stomach. I made a tuna noodle casserole and some fresh bread."

I felt she wanted to talk to me, so I politely accepted.

"Sure. That sounds good."

"Excellent. Go sit in the dining room, and I'll bring in the food."

I did as she asked and sat at a small round table that sat two. I couldn't believe Kate had already left. That right there indicated that she wanted to get away from me as quickly as possible.

"By the way, my name is Rose." She smiled as she set down my plate in front of me.

"It's a pleasure to meet you, Rose."

I placed the white cloth napkin on my lap as she sat down across from me.

"Do you know where Kate went?" I asked.

"I sent her back home to New York."

"Really?" I asked with excitement in my voice.

"You need to listen to me, Gabriel. If you want her back, give her time and space."

"But—"

"No buts." She held up her finger. "Kate needs time to figure herself out. I told her that running from her life wasn't the answer and that she should stay in New York because that's where her home and her father are. Kate and I talked every day. Sometimes for hours. She told me about her past, her father, and the circumstances that led to the two of you meeting and being reunited. She also told me what lengths she went to in order to give you your father's dream back. She said she did it for herself, to right all the wrongs she had done. But deep down inside, she did it for you because she loves you."

"And I love her."

"I know you do. I could see it in your eyes when you saw her standing on the stairs, and you found her here, in this small town of Mystic, when she could have been anywhere else in the world. I have hope for the two of you, but you must proceed cautiously."

"I don't understand." I frowned.

"In order to get back what the two of you had, you must start all over. Erase the past and everything that had happened. Lay the foundation for a new relationship. Reintroduce yourself to her as if you're meeting her for the first time. Get to know her without any judgment. Date her and take things slow. But she will need time. I know that may be difficult for you to hear, but it is essential that she's in a good place first."

"How long are we talking?" I asked.

"That's up to Kate."

"And what if she still wants nothing to do with me? She's the most important thing in my life."

"She still loves you, Gabriel, and she always will. Don't worry about the small things. Time is on both of your sides."

"How did you become so wise, Rose?" I smiled.

"I've lived a long time, dear, and I've experienced a lot in my life. I know what works and what doesn't. Now that you've finished your lunch, it's time for you to head home." She grinned. "I've made you a special care package of my famous homemade oatmeal chocolate chip cookies to take with you."

We both stood up from our seats, and I walked around to Rose and hugged her.

"Thank you, and thank you for taking care of Kate."

"You're welcome, dear. Make sure to keep in touch."

"I will." I smiled as I left the bed and breakfast.

Chapter Forty

Gabriel

A month and a half had passed since my conversation with Rose. I found it difficult to do as she said, but I did and stayed away from Kate. But that didn't mean I didn't follow her or, as Caleb would call it, stalk her to ensure she was okay. I also did it because I couldn't go that long without seeing her. Caleb met her once a week at a coffee shop and kept me posted about what was going on in her life. He hated betraying her confidence like that, but he knew how worried I was about her. She never asked Caleb about me, which hurt in some ways. Maybe she was over me and didn't care. Or maybe she was too afraid to ask. Either way, I was planning on making my move very soon.

～

K ate
My life was slowly getting back on track. I started my freelance art services thanks to a woman named Thea, whom I had met while browsing in an art gallery. We talked about a specific painting, and I told her I also painted. She was pregnant and asked me if I would paint a mural on the wall of her baby's nursery. She had been trying to find someone for a while, but her baby would already be born by the time someone was available to do it. I immediately took the job and finished it rather quickly since it was the only thing I had to do. She loved it so much and was so excited about it that she told her circle of friends, and they began calling me to do some artwork for them.

When I got home from Mystic, I did some house cleaning. I threw out all my wigs, passports, and anything and everything that had to do with a con. I was me now, Kate Harper, and she was the only person I'd ever be. As for Gabriel, I still thought about him every day, but as Rose promised, my heart was on the mend, and I didn't feel as sad anymore. It helped that I kept busy all day. It was the nighttime that was the loneliest.

I met with Caleb weekly for coffee and talked about my life and his. His recording career was taking off, and he traveled back and forth to L.A. a lot. I didn't ask about Gabriel, and he didn't talk about him. It was best that I didn't know what was going on in his life. I was sure he had found another woman by now. A man like him wouldn't go too long without dating. The thought saddened me, but it was for the best, and I realized that. I visited my father once a week, and he was thrilled that I decided to stay in New York. I told him about Rose, and he was happy I found someone like her. I didn't tell him that Gabriel had found me in Mystic. Some things were better off not being discussed. I felt that the more I talked about him, the harder it would be to get over what happened.

~

G abriel
I filed criminal charges against Thaddeus and Marcel. A court date was set for next month to decide their fate. My lawyer said chances were that Thaddeus would go to prison for espionage and theft since he took my plans and gave them to Marcel. The press had a field day with what had happened, and a majority of the company's shareholders pulled out and left the company in financial distress. Nothing had made me happier. I was getting anxious about Kate. The only problem was that since she was getting her life back on track, I was afraid I was nothing but a distant memory to her.

"I'm going to get Kate back, Grace," I spoke.

"And how are you going to do that?" She arched her brow.

"I have a plan." I grinned. "A good plan."

"I hope it works. I miss her." She smiled.

"I do too. Fingers crossed," I spoke as I got up from the island.

Chapter Forty-One

Kate

Weather permitting, I went to the lake in Central Park every Saturday morning, where I would spend at least an hour drawing or reading a book. Sometimes, I would stare into the water and appreciate the beauty surrounding me. A sense of peace and inspiration flowed through me every time, just like when I would sit in the gazebo in Mystic.

I sat on a wooden bench, sipping my coffee and staring at the lake as I thought about everything I had yet to do to get my business off the ground. My website was developing, and I still had to design and order some business cards. As I was sitting there, I caught something running towards me from the corner of my eye. Looking over, I saw it was a white puppy with a pink leash attached to it.

"Oh, my goodness. Where did you come from?" I smiled as I reached down to pet her.

She was a Maltese and the cutest little thing I had ever seen. I looked for tags on her collar but didn't see any. Then,

I looked around to see if anyone was coming to claim her. Obviously, she had gotten away from her owner.

"You are adorable." I picked her up and brought her nose to mine. "Where's your parents?"

She began licking my face over and over.

"Thank you for the kisses, sweet girl."

Suddenly, I heard a voice approach me from the side.

"There you are, you little rascal."

I looked over and saw Gabriel standing there. I felt my almost mended heart crack and a sick feeling washed over me.

"This is your dog?" I asked with suspicion as I narrowed my eyes at him.

"She is." He smiled at me. "We were walking, and she somehow broke free from my hand. Thank you for holding on to her. I'm Gabriel Quinn." He extended his hand.

I was confused as fuck as to what was happening, but I decided to play along.

"Kate Harper." I lightly shook his hand.

"It's nice to meet you, Kate."

"Likewise." I cocked my head.

"She likes you." He smiled as the dog wouldn't stop licking my face.

"She's adorable. How long have you had her?"

"A couple of days."

"What's her name? You really should get tags for her."

"I was going to, but I haven't named her yet."

"Why?" I asked in confusion.

"Because I haven't thought of a fitting name for her. Any suggestions?" He smirked.

"Well, growing up, I always wanted a white Maltese, and I was going to name her Lady because she's prim and proper." A small smile crossed my lips as I held the dog up and stared at her.

"I like it. Come on, Lady. We need to continue our walk."

I set the dog down and handed the leash to Gabriel. I could literally feel the crack in my heart begin to heal. Seeing him with that puppy gave me all the feels.

"Thank you again, Kate. It was a pleasure to meet you." The corners of his mouth curved into a smile as he walked away. Suddenly, he stopped and turned to me. "Excuse me, Kate?"

"Yes?"

"Would you, by any chance, like to join Lady and me on our walk?"

I couldn't help but smile at his invitation. "Sure. I would love to."

My head told me not to do it, but my heart told me it was okay.

We walked side by side through the park while Lady walked ahead of us. We talked as if we had just met for the first time, and I couldn't help but feel overjoyed at what he was doing. I told him about my business, and he told me about his. We talked about wine, food, our likes, and our dislikes. We laughed just like we used to, and our shared connection felt stronger than ever. Once we reached the main street, Gabriel stopped and turned to me.

"Thank you for joining us. Is there a chance I could get your phone number, and maybe we could go out some-time?" He smiled.

"I would like that."

He pulled his phone from his pocket and entered my number as I rattled it off. I said goodbye to Lady, and Gabriel walked away in the opposite direction I was going. I hesitated for a moment, and then the words just fell out of my mouth.

"Hey, Gabriel?" I called out to him.

"Yeah?" He stopped and looked at me.

"I don't have any plans tonight," I nervously spoke.

"Neither do I." He grinned. "Would you like to go to dinner and maybe catch a movie?"

"Yeah. I would." I bit down on my bottom lip.

He pulled his phone back out of his pocket.

"What's your address? I'll pick you up at six o'clock."

~

Gabriel

I let out a sigh of relief as I walked away from her. It worked. My plan worked. She was back in my life, and I was the happiest man alive. As soon as I climbed into the limo, I called Caleb.

"Hey, bro."

"I have a date tonight, Caleb. Kate and I are going to dinner and a movie."

"Thank God." He sighed. "I didn't know how much longer I was going to be able to put up with you."

I let out a chuckle.

"Let me guess. The dog?"

"Yeah. She couldn't resist her."

"I'm happy for you, Gabriel. Just do me a favor and don't be a fucking idiot this time."

"I won't be. I'm never letting her go again."

I ended the call and headed home. I took Lady upstairs with me as I gave Rose a call.

"The Mermaid Inn of Mystic, Rose speaking. How can I help you?"

"Rose, it's Gabriel."

"Hello, Gabriel. How are you?"

"I'm great. I just wanted to call you and let you know that Kate and I are going on a date tonight."

"What wonderful news. I'm so happy to hear that."

"Thanks, Rose, and again, thank you for your advice. I appreciate it."

"You're welcome, dear. I hope you and Kate have a great night together. Just remember, don't rush into anything. Take it slow and get to know each other all over again."

"I will. I'm not doing anything to potentially push her away."

Chapter Forty-Two

K ate

When I got home, I jumped on the couch and called Rose.

"The Mermaid Inn of Mystic, this is Rose. How may I help you?"

"Rose, it's me."

"Kate, darling. How are you?"

"I'm great. You're never going to believe where I'm going tonight."

"Where?"

"To dinner and a movie with Gabriel."

"Aw, Kate. That's wonderful news."

"You should have seen him today. He got a dog!" I spoke with excitement. "And we met in the park, and he introduced himself as if I were some stranger. Then I went for a walk with him and Lady, and we talked like we had never even known each other. It was so bizarre."

"I'm so happy for you, dear. Have a wonderful date with him, and I want to hear all about it tomorrow," she spoke.

"I will. I'll be in touch soon."

It was almost six o'clock when the buzzer to my apartment rang. Pressing the button to unlock the door, I stood in the doorway and waited for him to step off the elevator. When he did, I noticed he held a bouquet of flowers in his hand.

"You look beautiful." He smiled.

"Thank you. Come on in."

"These are for you." He handed me the beautiful red roses.

"Thank you, but you shouldn't have," I spoke as I brought them up to my nose and smelled them.

"I wanted to," he spoke with seriousness.

Our eyes met, and instantly, all the reasons why I fell in love with him before came flooding back. We went to dinner and talked so much that we missed the movie we were going to see. As we exited the restaurant, Gabriel took hold of my hand and looked at me, waiting to see if I would pull away. I didn't. All I did was smile, letting him know that it was okay. We walked down the brightly lit streets of New York and stopped in Orange Leaf for some frozen yogurt, where we talked some more and laughed before he took me home.

Gabriel walked me up to my apartment, and I invited him in for a glass of wine.

"Would you like to come in for a glass of wine?"

"As tempting as that sounds, I better get home to relieve the sitter."

"The sitter?" I asked.

"I have a dog sitter looking after Lady."

"Are you serious?" I laughed.

"Of course I am. She's just a baby. She can't be left home all alone."

My heart melted when he said that, and I suddenly lost control. I reached up and smashed my mouth against his. He placed his hands firmly on each side of my face as our passionate kiss continued. His warm lips pressed against mine were intoxicating, and I never wanted it to end. He broke our kiss and stared at me.

"We shouldn't. It's our first date."

"I don't care. I feel like I've been on a million dates with you already."

"Are you sure?"

"Yes. Are you?" I asked.

"It's all I ever think about. I've missed you so much, Kate."

"I've missed you too, Gabriel."

"Go pack a bag and come to my house with me. Lady will be happy to see you again."

I bit down on my bottom lip as excitement soared through me. I ran into the bedroom, threw some essentials into my bag, and we headed out the door.

Gabriel

She shocked me with that kiss, but it was a shock that felt so good and right. As soon as we arrived back at my townhouse, Lady came running to the door to greet us. Kate got down on the floor and played with her. As much as I wasn't a dog lover, I knew getting Lady was the right decision. Plus, she was already starting to grow on me, and seeing Kate with her made it all worth it.

I took her bag upstairs to my bedroom and set it on the chair. Kate followed, holding Lady in her arms. I turned to her and ran the back of my hand down her cheek.

"What do we do with Lady?" she asked.

"I'll take her down to her crate. She'll be fine for a while." I smiled.

After putting the dog downstairs, I returned to my room, where I found Kate sitting on the edge of the bed in a piece of lingerie I had bought her. She was exceptional and stunning, and my cock enjoyed the view as much as my eyes did. Walking over to her, I pushed her hair to the side and let my tongue slide across the delicate skin of her neck. She let out a light moan, the type of moan that I missed hearing. My hands traveled to her breasts as I caressed them through the sheer fabric of her nightie. My cock was so hard it hurt, and I couldn't wait to feel the warmth of her once again.

I gently laid her down on her back and removed the nightie from her perfect body. A body that I craved and missed for what seemed like an eternity. Our lips meshed with one another's as my hand traveled down the front of her panties and my finger dipped inside. She gasped and arched her back in pleasure, and I explored her. The wetness that emerged from her made me hungrier than I already was. I played with her and teased her hardened nipples with my tongue until she orgasmed. I licked every inch of her bare skin until I reached her wet sensitive spot. To taste her again was a dream come true. My tongue made tiny circles around her clit, heightening her arousal even more. Her moans became louder as her fingers ran through my hair. This was my piece of heaven.

I hovered over her, kissing her lips as I prepared to thrust inside her. The moment I'd been waiting for. I stared into her eyes as I broke our kiss, and my cock slowly entered inside. Her lips parted as a light gasp escaped her.

"I love you, Kate," I whispered as I buried myself inside her.

"I love you too, Gabriel." She smiled.

Chapter Forty-Three

Kate

I lay there, wrapped in his arms, feeling safe, secure, and happy while my body tried to come down from the multiple orgasms he had given me, my skin still trembling from his touch.

"Can I ask you something?" he spoke.

"Of course, you can." My finger gently ran along his chest.

"Promise me you won't get mad. Do you promise?"

"You want to know if I slept with Marcel. Don't you?"

"How did you know?"

"Because if the situation were reversed, I'd want to know." I lifted my head from his chest and touched his cheek. "No, I didn't sleep with him. I never had any intention to."

"And he was okay with that? He has a reputation."

"He had no choice. I told him I was on my period." I smiled.

He brought his hand up and ran his fingers through my hair.

"How did you get what you needed without him becoming suspicious?"

"You really want to know the truth?"

"I do, Kate. It's important that I know," he spoke with seriousness.

"I drugged him," I answered with a twisted face. "Put him to sleep for a while."

He stared at me in shock, but I knew he was proud.

"Thank you for doing what you did. Had I known, I would have stopped you. You took a huge risk, sweetheart."

"You're so cute for thinking you could have stopped me." I kissed the tip of his nose. "Anyway, you're welcome."

"I never meant a word of what I said to you that night at the ball. I was just so hurt and angry that you were with him."

"I know you were. But that's all in the past, and that's where it's staying."

"I love you so damn much. The thought that I had lost you forever killed me inside." His grip around me tightened.

Suddenly, we heard Lady barking from downstairs.

"Oh shit. I forgot about her," Gabriel spoke. "I'll be right back."

He climbed out of bed, pulled on his pajama bottoms, and left the room. I slipped into my nightie, grabbed my phone, and held it up to snap a picture when he walked back into the room. A few moments later, he returned with Lady in his arms.

"Freeze!" I exclaimed. "I want to get a picture."

"Now?" he asked.

"Smile." I smiled as I took a couple of pictures.

He set Lady down on the bed, and she ran up to me, giving me puppy kisses galore. Gabriel climbed into bed, and we played with her until we wore her out.

"She's your dog, Kate. I bought her for you."

"What? Are you kidding me?"

"No. You told me that you always wanted a white Maltese growing up. So, I thought you should have one. But I will tell you that I have become quite fond of her already, and I'm not sure I can let you take her away from me."

"But you just said she was mine." I pouted.

"I would love for her to be our dog, and I think the solution to this little problem is that you'll have to move in with me so she can be with both of us all the time."

I didn't even have to ponder the idea. The thought of moving in with him, sleeping with him every night, and waking up to him every morning made me feel like the luckiest woman alive.

"I would love to move in with you. That's if you're sure you can handle living with me 24/7." I smiled.

"Oh, I can handle you. We lived together before, don't forget. Plus, I've never been so sure about anything in my life." His lips brushed against mine.

It had been a month since I moved into Gabriel's townhome, and my life was perfect. I finally met his mother, who had just returned from Europe, where she had been traveling for the past six months. I liked her, and she seemed to like me too. Caleb's music career took off when his song hit #5 on the music charts. He would go on tour in a few weeks, being the opening band for Matchbox Twenty. Lady was growing so fast, and Gabriel and I completely loved her.

I slipped into a short, red, form-fitting dress that sat off the shoulders for a special dinner Gabriel had planned for us.

"You look beautiful," he spoke as he walked up behind me and pressed his lips against my neck.

"Thank you." I smiled.

"I picked up a little something for you today." He pulled a small red box from his suit pocket and handed it to me.

Opening the lid, I gasped when I saw the beautiful princess-cut diamond earrings.

"Gabriel, they're beautiful. You shouldn't have. What is this for?"

"Yes, I should have, and they're just a reminder of how much I love you and how beautiful you are."

I started to fan my eyes to keep the tears from falling.

"Thank you. I love you so much." I threw my arms around his neck and kissed his lips.

"You're welcome. Are you almost ready? Our reservations are for seven."

"Yes. I have to put these earrings in, and then we can go." I smiled.

We arrived at his hotel, and I looked at him in confusion.

"We're eating at your hotel?" I asked.

"Yes." He smiled as he grabbed my hand and led me inside.

We entered Cornelia, the upscale restaurant in the hotel named after his mother. I looked around, for we were the only two people in the place.

"Good evening, Mr. Quinn. I'll show you to your table."

"Good evening, Frank."

"Gabriel, I'm confused. Why is nobody here?" I asked as I took a seat.

"I closed the restaurant down for tonight for a very special celebration."

"What are we celebrating?"

"Him." Gabriel held out his hand.

I looked behind me and saw my father, dressed in a black suit, standing there.

"Hello, baby girl." He smiled.

Throwing my hands over my mouth, I looked at Gabriel, who stood there with a smile on his face. I got up from my seat and ran over to my father, throwing my arms around him and hugging him tight.

"What are you doing here?" I asked.

"Why don't you ask Gabriel?"

I turned and looked at him, and suddenly, tears filled my eyes when I realized what he had done.

"Don't cry, baby," he spoke as he walked over to me and wiped the tears from my face.

"I can't believe you did this."

"Did you really think I would let him sit in prison? I'd been waiting for this night for a while. I wanted to surprise you, and keeping this a secret was so hard."

"God, Gabriel. I love you so much. Thank you."

"I love you too, baby."

The three of us sat down and enjoyed a wonderful dinner together. Gabriel had given my father a job at this hotel and a free room until he could save some money to afford an apartment. This, my life, was all too surreal. Having the two men who were my life's most important people at my side was like a dream come true.

Chapter Forty-Four

Three Months Later

Gabriel

"You have everything packed?" Kate asked as she walked into the bedroom.

"I do, baby. I wish you could come with me." I placed my hands firmly on her hips. "But I'm going to be tied up in various meetings for days."

"It's okay. I understand." She smiled.

"I'm happy you're going to visit Rose this weekend. I really didn't want you to be here all alone."

"I can't wait to see her, and she finally gets to meet Lady."

I brushed my lips against hers and hugged her tightly.

"I'm going to miss you," I whispered in her ear.

"I'm going to miss you too. Try not to work too hard."

"I promise to call you every day and expect many text messages from me."

"I look forward to each and every one. I love you, Gabriel."

"I love you too, baby." I gave her one last kiss and took my suitcase downstairs.

The truth was that I had to fly to Boston for a planning meeting for a few hours. After finishing that, I would fly to Mystic to surprise her.

~

K ate

It felt good to be back in Mystic again. Rose greeted me with open arms and fell in love with Lady the minute she saw her.

"I'm so happy you're here." She smiled.

"Me too."

"Bobby is going to cover the bed and breakfast for me today while I spend the entire day with you and this little lady."

We spent the day shopping, had lunch, walked on the trails, and then headed back. I noticed the dining room doors were shut when we arrived at the bed and breakfast. Rose never kept them closed.

"Ah, good. You're back." Bobby smiled. "I went ahead and made dinner for you."

"Aw, Bobby, you shouldn't have," Rose spoke. "Kate, why don't you go into the dining room and have a seat? I will take Lady outside and see if she has to go potty."

I smiled at her as I opened the dining room doors. I froze when I saw Gabriel standing near a beautifully decorated table lit with candles and arranged with fresh flowers.

"Oh, my God, what are you doing here?" I asked with shock as I walked over and wrapped my arms around him. "What happened to your meetings?"

"I already had my meeting."

"Huh? I don't understand. You said that you would be tied up for a few days." I broke our embrace.

"I am going to be tied up for a few days, but not with meetings," he spoke. "Kate, sit down."

"Gabriel, what's going on?"

He got down on one knee and pulled a small box from his pocket. Opening the lid, he took out a beautiful diamond ring and held it up.

"Kate, words cannot explain how much you have changed my life. I never thought I would love someone as much as I love you. You are my entire world, and I can't imagine you not being in it."

I placed my hand over my mouth as tears started to stream down my face.

"Living with you the past three months has been incredible, and I fall in love with you more every single day. I didn't think it was possible, but I do, and I want to spend the rest of my life with you as your husband and you as my wife. Being my girlfriend just isn't enough for me. Will you do me the honor of marrying me and spending the rest of your life as Mrs. Gabriel Quinn?"

The uncontrollable urge to bawl my eyes out swept over me as I cried like a baby in front of him.

"Sweetheart, you're scaring me."

"I—I—I'm just so happy," I cried. "I wasn't expecting this."

"I wanted to surprise you. So—"

"Yes! Of course, I'll marry you. It's all I want."

A wide grin splayed across his face as he slipped the ring on my finger and brought my hand to his lips.

"I love you more than life, baby," he spoke.

I was shaking uncontrollably as I wrapped my arms around his neck, and we stood up.

"I love you more than life," I whispered in his ear.

Suddenly, we heard the light claps of Bobby and Rose,

who stood in the doorway and watched us. Rose set Lady down, and she came running over to us. Gabriel bent down and picked her up.

"She said yes, Lady. Your mama said yes!" he spoke with excitement.

"Looks like we have a wedding to plan, Bobby." Rose smiled.

"We sure do, Rose." He hooked his arm around her as she laid her head on his shoulder.

G abriel and I were married in the gazebo at The Mermaid Inn of Mystic. I couldn't have asked for a more beautiful day. The sun was shining, and it was a perfect seventy-five degrees outside. We had to plan the wedding quite quickly while the weather was still nice, which was fine with me because I couldn't wait to become Mrs. Gabriel Quinn. We kept the wedding small, inviting only about a hundred people. It was what we both wanted. Something intimate with family and a few friends.

"Welcome to the family." Caleb smiled as he kissed my cheek and hugged me.

"Thanks, Caleb."

"Welcome to the family, Kate. I couldn't have asked for a better woman for my son to marry." His mother grinned.

Gabriel and I decided not to tell her about my past, and we warned my father not to speak of his. She would be appalled and change her mind about me if she knew how we really met.

Gabriel

I had never felt so much happiness in my life. It was time for us to have our first dance together as husband and wife. As soon as Caleb and his band began to play, I took Kate's hand and led her to the dance floor in the middle of the huge white tent strung with white lights, decorated tables and chairs, and fresh flowers that made it look exquisite. Rose had really outdone herself for our special day.

"Have I told you how beautiful you look today?" I smiled as I held Kate close to me.

"About a hundred times. But you can keep telling me." She grinned.

"You don't have to worry about that. I will spend my life telling you how beautiful you are." His lips brushed against mine.

"You know, we never discussed how many kids we want to have," she spoke. "Do you even want children?"

"Of course, I do, and I think two or three is a good number. What do you think?" He smirked.

"I think two or three is perfect. Maybe we could agree on two, and then if it happens a third time, that would be okay."

"I like that idea." I pressed my forehead against hers.

"Is nine months too soon?" She bit down on her bottom lip.

I stared at her momentarily, then leaned in and whispered, "Are you trying to tell me something?"

"I'm pregnant, Gabriel. I took the test this morning. I thought maybe I was just late because of all our planning for the wedding."

I slowly closed my eyes, pulled her closer, and held her against me.

"I am so happy, and the thought of you carrying my child just made everything more perfect."

"So you're happy?" she asked as she pulled away from me slightly.

"Happy isn't the word to describe what I'm feeling right now. I can't wait to hold our baby and raise a family together."

～

I had become the proud father of Elijah Matthew Quinn, the future heir to Quinn Hotels. Finally, my dream of raising a family in my townhome had come true. Just when I had given up on finding the woman of my dreams, Kate Harper walked into my life and gave me the two most precious gifts of all: love and my son. My life was complete, and I wouldn't take any of it for granted.

"Come on, Elijah. Walk to Daddy." I smiled as I held my arms to him from across the living room.

Kate slowly let go of him, and he took a few steps toward me before he fell to his knees and crawled the rest of the way into my arms.

"Good job, buddy. You'll get it soon enough." I picked him up and kissed his head. "I can't believe he's going to be a year old tomorrow." A smile crossed my face as I walked over to where Kate sat on the couch.

"I know. He's growing up so fast." She pouted.

"Before you know it, we'll be free of diapers and bottles. Now that he's sleeping through the entire night, we can get some good sleep for ourselves." I smirked as I kissed her lips.

She looked at me and bit down on her bottom lip.

"I wouldn't get too used to that if I were you."

"Kate, are you trying to tell me something?" I asked as my brow arched.

She threw her hands up in the air with a smile.

"Woohoo! I'm pregnant again!"

I set Elijah down on the floor and wrapped my arms around her as excitement and joy overtook me.

"A beautiful wife, a beautiful son, and another baby on the way. Life is good, Kate. Really good." I kissed the side of her head. "We've been so blessed."

"We sure have, Gabriel. I love you and our little family so much."

"I love us too. More than words could ever express." I placed my hand on her belly.

Thank you for reading The Con Artist! I hope you enjoyed it!

Be sure to check out More Sizzling Romance!

I invite you to join my Sandi's Romance Readers Facebook Group, where we talk about books, romance, and more! Come join the fun!

Newsletter
Website
Facebook
Instagram

Sandi Lynn

FOLLOW ME ON AMAZON
TikTok
Bookbub
Goodreads

More Sizzling Romance

Looking for more romance reads about billionaires, second chances, and sports? Check out my other romance novels and escape to another world and from the daily grind of life – one book at a time.

Series:

Forever Series
Forever Black (Forever, Book 1)
Forever You (Forever, Book 2)
Forever Us (Forever, Book 3)
Being Julia (Forever, Book 4)
Collin (Forever, Book 5)
A Forever Family (Forever, Book 6)
A Forever Christmas (Holiday short story)

Wyatt Brothers
Love, Lust & A Millionaire (Wyatt Brothers, Book 1)
Love, Lust & Liam (Wyatt Brothers, Book 2)

More Sizzling Romance

A Millionaire's Love
Lie Next to Me (A Millionaire's Love, Book 1)
When I Lie with You (A Millionaire's Love, Book 2)

Happened Series
Then You Happened (Happened Series, Book 1)
Then We Happened (Happened Series, Book 2)

Redemption Series
Carter Grayson (Redemption Series, Book 1)
Chase Calloway (Redemption Series, Book 2)
Jamieson Finn (Redemption Series, Book 3)
Damien Prescott (Redemption Series, Book 4)

Interview Series
The Interview: New York & Los Angeles Part 1
The Interview: New York & Los Angeles Part 2

Love Series:
Love In Between (Love Series, Book 1)
The Upside of Love (Love Series, Book 2)

Wolfe Brothers
Elijah Wolfe (Wolfe Brothers, Book 1)
Nathan Wolfe (Wolfe Brothers, Book 2)
Mason Wolfe (Wolfe Brothers, Book 3)

Kind Brothers
One of a Kind (Kind Brothers Series, Book 1)
Two of a Kind (Kind Brothers Series, Book 2)
Three of a Kind (Kind Brothers Series, Book 3)
Four of a Kind (Kind Brothers Series, Book 4)
Five of a Kind (Kind Brothers Series, Book 5)

The Kind Brothers (Kind Brothers Series, Book 6)
Six of a Kind (Kind Brothers Series, Book 7)
Seven of a Kind (Kind Brothers Series, Book 8)
Eight of a Kind (Kind Brothers Series, Book 9)
Nine of a Kind (Kind Brothers Series, Book 10)
A Kind Wedding: Jackson & Georgia (Kind Brothers Series, Book 11)
A Kind Wedding: Conner & Charlotte (Kind Brothers Series, Book 12)
A Kind Wedding: Nathan & Sofia (Kind Brothers Series, Book 13)
A Kind Wedding: Christian & Charleigh (Kind Brothers Series, Book 14)
Ten of a Kind (Kind Brothers Series, Book 15)
Eleven of a Kind (Kind Brothers Series, Book 16)
Twelve of a Kind (Kind Brothers Series, Book 17)
Thirteen of a Kind (Kind Brothers Series, Book 18)
Fourteen of a Kind (Kind Brothers Series, Book 19)

One Night Series:
One Night In London
One Night in Paris

Broken Hearts Series
Unspoken
A Beautiful Sight
When I'm With You

Baby Drama Series
Baby Drama
Baby Drama II
Baby Drama III

More Sizzling Romance

Harbor Falls Series
Love In Harbor Falls
Only You

Standalone Books

The Billionaire's Christmas Baby
His Proposed Deal
The Secret He Holds
The Seduction of Alex Parker
Something About Lorelei
The Exception
Corporate Assets
The Negotiation
Defense
The Con Artist
#Delete
Behind His Lies
Perfectly You
The Escort
The Ring
The Donor
Rewind
Remembering You
LOGAN (A Hockey Romance)
The Merger
The Property Brokers
Unwrapping Romance

Printed in Great Britain
by Amazon